For Jan

With [...]

from

Julian

26 February 1981

GENTLEMAN'S GENTLEMAN

By the same author

MORNING
A LETTER
MEMOIR IN THE MIDDLE OF THE JOURNEY
GABRIEL YOUNG
TUG-OF-WAR
HOUNDS OF SPRING
HAPPY ENDINGS
REVOLUTION ISLAND

JULIAN FANE

Gentleman's Gentleman

HAMISH HAMILTON
and ST GEORGE'S PRESS

First published in Great Britain 1981
by Hamish Hamilton Ltd
Garden House 57–59 Long Acre London WC2E 9JZ
and St George's Press Ltd
37 Manchester Street Baker Street London W1M 5PE

British Library Cataloguing in Publication Data
Fane, Julian
 Gentleman's gentleman.
 I. Title
 823'.9'1F
 ISBN 0–241–10604–4

Printed in Great Britain by
Willmer Brothers Limited, Rock Ferry, Merseyside

TO CARLO ARDITO

1

William Kitchener Brown died last October, between the ninth and the sixteenth days of the month, at the age of sixty-three or sixty-four or sixty-five.

He was always secretive.

For thirty-odd years he was the manservant, butler, cook, valet, general factotum, jester and boon companion of my old friend and fellow-writer Hereward Watkins.

You have to be famous to merit any sort of biography, let alone a biography embarked upon a few weeks after your death. The following anecdote is a measure of the fame of William Kitchener Brown, alias Bill, Billy, Kitch, for some unknown reason Terry, and Brownie.

A resident of Dundee, a retired nurse acquainted with Hereward, was introduced to a couple of young New Zealanders who were touring the British Isles. She had previously lived in London and said so, whereupon they exclaimed: 'In that case you must know Brownie!' She was amused by their assumption; referred to the millions of Londoners and thousands of Browns; but admitted that in the metropolis she had known one particular Mr Brown, often called Brownie; and having satisfied herself that they were talking about the same man, asked where they had come across him.

I

'In pubs,' they replied. 'He's a wonderful character. He kept us in fits of laughter with imitations of his boss.'

Hereward was not surprised to hear he was the chief butt of Brownie's jokes with strangers. He used to complain that he could scarcely look his neighbours in the eye because he was sure his reputation had been ruined.

But let me describe my hero – or rather heroes.

My friend is now in his early fifties, tall, thin as ever, not to say gaunt. Although his narrow face is remarkably unlined, his hair is grey and scanty. With his long inquisitive novelist's nose he resembles a benevolent heron. In those books of his which he narrates in the first person he pretends to be middle-class – actually a fib, or poetic licence, or an expression of literary tact in an egalitarian era, or inverted snobbery. If he had been middle-class, Brownie would never have worked for him for thirty years. Hereward, as his Christian name may imply, was born an aristocrat: he has given me permission to reveal the shameful truth essential to my present undertaking. He can trace his lineage to barbarous Welsh antiquity. His family home is Watkins Hall, a stately pile in the Brecon Beacons.

Nobody should wonder that he and his manservant got on so well together – extremes touch, after all. Brownie was reared in the humblest circumstances in the dark interior of South-east London. To begin with he reminded me of films of the Great War – the 1914 war – showing stunted, wiry, invincibly cocky and cheery private soldiers marching, cooking, fooling about and chatting up the local populace. He was the same Tommy Atkins type, the quick-witted Cockney personified, irreverent, amoral, ever ready to laugh at life and at death, eternally making the best of things. At that time, when I met him, he was thirty-ish. His head was more square-shaped than round – he had a squared top to his fore-head. His fine straight hair was light mouse-colour : he parted what remained of it in the middle, brushed it flat and back, and had it clipped short, army style. His eyes tended to protrude. His features were fleshy and formless. He would have defeated an Identikit artist not only because his whole appearance seemed to be ordinary, also because he could change it at will.

Later he put on a lot of weight. His chins doubled and his belly burst out of his shirts. He cursed the manufacturers of his tight trousers : 'They cut them for queers nowadays.' But at a party in his white jacket he could still hold himself in and boast he was broad-shouldered and not broad in the beam. Strutting off for a weekend visit to relations, wearing a suit with knife-edge creases, brightly polished shoes, a spotless blue overcoat, a black trilby at a rakish angle, and carrying a rolled umbrella, he could play the part of a perfect gentleman's gentleman. His repertoire of roles was inex-haustible : he should have been a professional actor or comedian. He would don his oldest dirtiest clothes and shamble along unshaven to tell a hard-line tale to his Tax Inspector. He twisted doctors round his stubby little finger. As for his ordinary face, from one moment to the next it expressed rosy shiny good health, chronic sickness and debility, deep respect for his social superiors and radical scorn, a touching desire to please his master and long-suffering resentment of the way he was being exploited, simple-hearted frankness, wily sophistication, fastidious refinement, stunning vulgarity, and so on.

He was purest mercury and never to be taken too seriously. He was bored by woe, repetition, accuracy, sincerity. He really lived for laughs.

Yet he was a golden person as well as mercurial. His vocation, arguably the highest, was to look after others.

What could be more complimentary than those twin epitaphs?

Perhaps he was bound to fall foul of the occupational hazard of extremely kind sociable sensitive people and especially menservants: in short, drink. He fought against it. At least he said he fought against it. And Hereward was drawn into the fight, despite his appreciation of the irony of the situation – no doubt Hereward did most of the fighting. Thus, notwithstanding his natural abstemiousness, and indeed his asceticism on principle, he was engaged in a vicarious losing battle with drunkenness for three decades.

One day somebody consoled him: 'Don't worry – when Brownie's in heaven and you're knocking on the pearly gates, he may put in a good word for you.'

Whether or not Brownie has wangled himself the ultimately comfortable billet remains to be seen. And even if he was not famous in the full worldly sense, although two tourists from New Zealand were quite right to assume an ex-Londoner in Dundee must know him, he deserves to be commemorated – along with his jokes.

Moreover he meant to write his autobiography. My book aims to be a representative token of the esteem and gratitude of his boss's various guests, whom he welcomed and fed and helped to entertain unforgettably – and a second-hand or third-hand substitute for his.

Hereward has promised to supply me with the necessary biographical material, which he feels he could never be objective enough to use. He is resigning the copyright he inherited from Brownie in my favour.

Co-operate as we may, rack our bookish brains as we may,

the trouble is that the title of our tribute will not be a patch on Brownie's.

He planned to call his reminiscences: *Bad Manners And Peculiar Habits Of The Upper Crust.*

*

His mother was Scottish and worked as a charwoman in Kent.

I am quoting Brownie: gentle readers should therefore abandon hope of consequential logic.

His mother married twice and produced hordes of children, Brownie being the youngest of the second family – I suppose she began by marrying an Englishman and that they settled in Plumstead in Kent.

But immediately the plot thickens. Although Plumstead is not within range of the sound of Bow Bells, Brownie qualified as a Cockney in many other respects. He was not merely the Tommy Atkins type, his native speech was Cockney, he was familiar with Cockney rhyming slang, he excelled at repartee Cockney-fashion – he was like Shakespeare's clever clowns with their pavement wit. Nevertheless his mother was definitely Scottish – and then he confided in Hereward that his father was Austrian.

'I should spell my name with an *a* and a *u* in the middle instead of an *o* and a *w*,' he stated rather proudly, for he admired the Teutonic race, its efficiency, its punctuality.

How an Austrian met and married a Scottish widow in Plumstead, and lived and sired children there during the First World War, when Austria was our enemy, I cannot imagine.

Brownie was no more than rather proud of his father. He

was apt to dismiss the subject by saying: 'He died before I knew him.' He was a trifle uneasy about his parentage.

'One of us was illegitimate – or so they said. We were never sure which it was – probably one of my half-brothers or half-sisters. But they were all little bastards.'

'Could it be you, Brownie?'

'No, sir!' His pronunciation became military: 'No, SAH!' He emphasised the 'SAH!' in his old soldier's accents whenever he wanted to convey strong disagreement. 'No, sir! Would you like to see my birth certificate, sir? It's signed and sealed and above board – SAH!'

In fact he was tickled by Hereward's suggestion that he might be the little bastard, which was the more outrageous in the context of the severe working-class attitude towards bastardy. He revelled in outrageousness, even when he was on the receiving end of it.

But Hereward could have been closer to the truth than he knew. For Brownie was born in 1914 or 1915 or 1916. And supposing an Austrian called Braun married his mother, would not the said Braun have gone home or perhaps been recalled to his colours as soon as war was declared? If he had remained here, would he not have been interned as an alien, unless he was naturalised, in which case he would have served in the British army? Would he have been so patriotic for the country of his adoption as to christen his son Kitchener?

The circumstances of Brownie's paternity were characteristically ambiguous. His offer to produce his birth certificate was merely a red herring: the document would automatically include the name of his mother's husband, absent or present: it would not decide on which side of the blanket he had been conceived. Yet, while it is tempting to believe he was what

6

he seemed to be, that is the Cockney offspring of a Kentish Cockney father who committed adultery in Plumstead, doubts again creep in with recollections of his square forehead and the roll of flesh at the nape of his neck, which would have fitted snugly under a *pickelhaube*.

To confuse the issue further, he also claimed he had gipsy blood in his veins.

'I'm part Romany. I like to eat roast hedgehog and I don't like hot baths. We Romanys are against baths because they wash off our precious body-oils.'

For that matter he claimed he was a rat-catcher – R.C. or Roman Catholic: which would reinforce the theory that he was half-Austrian.

At any rate I feel sure his mother was Scottish. After the death or disappearance of her second spouse whoever he was, she presided over her brood and taught it how to behave. Her justice was rough: at meals, should any child reach out rudely for food, she would spear the offending hand with her fork. She had to slave at her charwoman's work in order to provide for the fatherless family. She earned the respect of her landlord, who bought and brought her an occasional glass of stout from the pub.

Brownie, her last baby, possibly a love-child, and possessed of winning ways into the bargain, was her favourite. In return he revered her memory. Home was crowded, although some of the older children had already married and left it. Brownie shared a single bed with two teenage sisters, Evie and Ada, lying with his head between their feet until he was fourteen or so. He may have developed his antipathy to hot baths when he was forced to have them in a hip-bath in public in front of the kitchen stove.

He was a wild lad with a shock of fair hair and a terrible temper by his own accounts. One day in school he lost his temper, threw an inkwell at his schoolmaster, knocked the schoolmaster's eye out, and was sent to a boys' reformatory. He was pretty miserable there for an unspecified period.

Then fortune smiled on him for maybe the first of many times. Somehow he got a job as a page in a grand London club.

Meanwhile his mother was dying. She suffered from a rare ailment which she passed on to her ewe lamb. Von Reckling-hausen's Disease causes fatty non-malignant tumours to form on the nerve endings. It is incurable, but not dangerous unless a tumour should inhibit a vital function. Apparently she got one on her optic nerve, and went blind and mad, owing to pressure on the brain, before it killed her.

Brownie would describe her death in such horrific detail that Hereward's initial sympathy was tempered by cynical suspicion. He was mourning his mother and protesting against her cruel fate, incidentally extracting a bit of black humour from his bereavement, and slipping a trump card up his sleeve. If he drank too much, he could plead the extenuating circumstance of fear of his heredity. He had a ready-made excuse in the shape of the ominous tumours bulging from his body.

Mrs Brown or Braun was buried in about 1930. She must have been kindly, brave in her poor widowhood, and appreciative of merit. Some of her children joined the Salvation Army. The others were sinners, according to Brownie's hints. He lost touch or quarrelled with all his siblings sooner or later.

*

He wore a page-boy's uniform at the Piccadilly Club in the street of the same name.

Once an old curmudgeon of a member complained that he had spied a page strolling along Piccadilly, whistling and with his hands in his pockets. Brownie was identified as the culprit and hauled in front of the club committee.

'What have you got to say for yourself?'

'Mr So-and-so made a mistake, sir!'

'What's that? Are you trying to be impertinent?'

'No, sir! But I can't whistle, sir. I never learnt how to whistle or spit. And my uniform doesn't have pockets – the side-seams of my trousers are sewn up to the waist!'

The case was dismissed. Brownie had scored another victory in the class war – or at least in his lifelong campaign against authority.

He was English through and through in his acute consciousness of class and his snobbery. He liked to work for, he felt he profited from being associated with, and actually enjoyed the company of gentlemen by his standards. He cultivated a manner of speaking that he believed was gentlemanly: as a result, unperceptive upper-class people thought he was a mincing homosexual when he mimicked their voices and airs and graces.

He used to tease Hereward by answering the telephone in his affected pretentious style: 'Hillow? Hillow – Mr Hereward Watkins' residence! . . . Oh, 'ullo, sir! It's you, is it? Yes, 'e's 'ere – 'ang on, I'll give him a shout.'

Either because he was intelligent, or because of the experience he gained at the Piccadilly, he arrived at an understanding of the interdependence of masters and servants. He was therefore never awed by his social superiors: he realised they needed him as much as he needed them.

'There are good 'uns and bads 'uns – they're like the rest of us, if you get to know them.'

On one level of his complexity he accepted the class system. On another it was material for his mocking jokes: 'Went to Eton, did he? I know – I can see it. He was eaten and brought up.' On a third he was poised to take cover behind the revolutionary barricades and open fire on the idle rich.

In spite of himself he was impressed by authoritarianism. Almost more than a lord, he loved an eccentric authoritarian plutocrat, whose bad manners and peculiar habits were amusing copy for the book he intended to write.

The Albanian oil millionaire Achmed Bogu was a member of the Piccadilly. He had as it were gone native in England and acquired a country seat, a pack of hounds, shooting and fishing, and a couple of dozen racehorses. In London he had breakfast in his club every morning. The ritual began by Brownie being despatched to buy a fresh peach and a fresh nectarine from Fortnum and Mason. Then at a quarter to nine sharp a Rolls-Royce drew up at the door and Mr Bogu's second chauffeur unloaded from it and carried downstairs to the club barber's shop the special chair in which Mr Bogu liked to have his beard attended to. At nine another Rolls-Royce driven by the head-chauffeur deposited Mr Bogu in person, who, after spending half an hour with the barber, appeared in the dining-room with his beard and his eyebrows trimmed and curled and his monocle in place. He sat at a table by a window and ate two kippers, several racks of toast and marmalade, followed by the peach and nectarine, and drank half a gallon of potent coffee and cream.

Naturally Brownie was chosen by Mr Bogu to serve breakfast: he had risen in the staff hierarchy of the club from page to waiter by this time. His boast that he was always chosen to wait on the most demanding members was probably justified: he was so quick, willing and eager to please, and his trick of remembering and indulging their individual fads was so flattering. Moreover he liked to practise the sport at which he excelled, as we all do : in his case it was taming fierce establishment lions and – nearly literally – training them to feed out of his hand.

For instance Sir Gervaise Such-and-such would eat nothing but a slice of paper-thin brawn and a baked potato in the middle of the day; the Marquis of Somewhere had to have pepper within reach to sprinkle on his strawberries; an apocryphal Count Nudel drank warm water with a meal, whereas Admiral Lord Hamish McNaught stuck to pink gins – none of them needed to remind Brownie of these require-ments. The Earl of Grimlingham, notorious for his evil temper, a wife-batterer and a scourge of club servants, could not bear to have any waiter near him except Brownie : who decided His Lordship was lonely, which was to be expected, and quite sweet.

Of course the source of my information was Brownie himself. Paradoxically it was proof of his modesty that he published every compliment he had ever been paid.

'The Earl of Grimlingham said I was the only young feller with any sense he'd given an order to in the whole of his life . . . Admiral Lord Hamish thought I took the ship's biscuit.'

Whether or not he exaggerated the praises of the innumer-able people he looked after is a moot point. But Hereward's opinion coincides with mine : such exaggeration would have been superfluous.

The Piccadilly seems to have had a more cosmopolitan membership than the other three clubs then in its vicinity, the Turf, the St James's and the Naval and Military. Brownie would say that Prince Everhazy, Duke Socci di Bocci, Graf von Twisch and Baron Rémy were members, as well as Count Nudel and Mr Bogu.

He adopted a heavy foreign accent when he reeled off the above list of names. He fancied himself as a linguist. His enunciation of the French title and surname, Baron Rémy, included the full glottal stops. He was partial to the glottal stop and inclined to introduce it into English words, pronouncing porridge por-h-ridge, for example.

The fact that the Piccadilly was a gambling club might have had something to do with its members from abroad. Brownie was excited by his turns of duty in the Card Room: he had no sociological objections to the size of the sums of money at stake. But it amazed him that the players talked and laughed and called for drinks in loud voices, while thousands of pounds were changing hands, whereas in the Billiards Room strict silence was the rule, although bets on a game were restricted to a maximum of five shillings.

One of his special pets amongst the members was Lord Charles Tatham, D.S.O. and Bar, known as Tatters. Tatters Tatham was a gambling man, a womaniser, an amateur jockey who had ridden in the Grand National, a celebrated wit and *bon viveur* in his day. He instructed his mistresses to telephone him at the club rather than at home, where they might get through to his wife. If – or when – a mistress rang and asked for Lord Charles, the telephone operator's drill was to say he was out, take a written message and pass it to Brownie, who would fold it carefully and carry it on a silver salver to the Card Room and slip it under his habitual tumbler of whisky and soda. Should Lord Charles really be out, Brownie would hang around in order to hand him his messages as discreetly as possible the minute he came in. The object of the exercise was threefold: to make sure Tatters was not interrupted at cards; to give him a chance to prepare his defence against the hysterical females he had treated in cavalier fashion; and to avoid the unpleasantness of his fellow-members' discovery that their own wives or daughters were compromised by being on the line.

Brownie told a good story illustrative of the wit of Tatters Tatham, who was temporarily engaged in an extra-marital affair with a certain Lady Grace Something-or-other.

He – Tatters – pulled a noticeably long face as he entered the club bar.

'What's up, old boy?' his cronies enquired. 'Have a hair of the dog that bit you!'

'No, thanks – nothing to drink – I've finally reformed.'

'What? You don't mean it! Reformed?'

'Yes – it's true – scout's honour! I've got religion. Nowadays I even have Grace before dinner.'

*

In the thirties, genuine English gentlemen and the would-be sort seem to have spent most of their lives with other gentlemen – at school, in the armed services, at work, in their sporting pursuits, and at mixed social gatherings in the evenings over port and cigars. Furthermore they gratified their apparently insatiable appetites for masculine company, or sought refuge from the opposite sex, in their exclusive clubs.

Yet historical documents attest that they distressed the ladies, and vice versa, as much as we do in our unisex epoch: where did they find the time?

The hall-porter at the Piccadilly, and his minions like Brownie, had to be careful not only about telephone calls. Wives and daughters who had run through their money out shopping would demand to see their husbands and fathers, or beg for a loan from the club's petty-cash-box. Importunate women would come and wait on the club steps for their elusive lovers. On several occasions an aggressively drunk girl with a grudge against a member tried to force an entry.

Brownie remembered a white-faced wife asking for her compulsive gambler of a spouse, and then sitting for hours in a car outside the club, her despairing eyes fixed on the front door. Again, he felt sorry for everyone concerned when some wretched young member was summoning the Dutch courage in the bar to go home and break the news to his family that he was ruined.

A little world so male-oriented was bound to be productive of homosexuality.

As Brownie put it: 'We had our share.'

He was convinced that he had been a pretty youth.

'Colonel Algy Poppin and Duke Socci di Bocci couldn't keep their hands off me,' he assured Hereward.

'Really? When did you lose your looks?'

'Thank you, sir. I never lost my looks – I just matured.'

'Well – when did you lose that mop of hair you say you used to have?'

'I shed my blood and my hair, fighting for king and country.'

'Who were the members that couldn't keep their hands off you?'

'Colonel Poppin and Duke Socci di Bocci. And Graf von Twisch – he was a holy terror.'

'Are you sure you've got those names right, Brownie?'

'Yes, sir.'

'They sound a bit funny to me.'

'They were funny gentlemen, sir!'

14

Colonel Poppin had lured Brownie into a telephone booth and attempted to kiss him. And Mr Gregory Nickson, called Mr Knicks-off below stairs, bribed page-boys to visit his flat, which was a few minutes' walk from the Piccadilly.

'Did you go?'

'No, sir! My mother wouldn't have liked it.'

Unmarried staff slept on the upper floors of the club premises. Brownie in his leisure hours went to films and music halls, and strolled round Shepherd Market. He made friends with an old fishmonger there, who taught him how to open oysters and skin and fillet fish, and with various prostitutes on an uncommercial basis. A prostitute named Ruby would take him to a pub in the area and buy him a supper of a baby's head – a delicious kind of circular steak and kidney pudding.

He was paid the merest pittance to start with, perhaps £1 per week. But he had no expenses and was well fed, even if he managed to give Ruby the impression he was starving.

'We ate the leftovers from the members' dining-room. We fed like fighting cocks.'

Almost always throughout his adult life he so arranged matters that he was fed like a fighting cock.

And then he received tips. The Piccadilly along with other clubs banned tipping; but no rules or regulations were going to stop a gentleman who could afford to be generous from showing his appreciation of first-class service. Nothing was ever too much trouble for Brownie – fetching, carrying, walking a member's dog, standing in a deluge of rain to hail a taxi. He was blessed with the sunniest of tempers and the still rarer gift of being able to cheer people up. Inevitably banknotes were pressed into his hand and, in the dining-room, found by him beneath the side-plates of the members he had waited on. At some stage he was honoured to become a so-called 'trusted servant': he worked either as or with the club cashier and was allotted the mysterious task of over-seeing the financial transactions in the Card Room. He was therefore handling large sums of money – and he benefited by often getting a cut of a gambler's winnings.

Moreover in due course he was permitted to open a Staff Beer Bar in a disused cellar, which must have been profitable. Later on he swore that no alcoholic beverage had passed his lips until after the war. But is it likely he could run a bar for beer without touching a drop? And where did he acquire his taste for port if not at the Piccadilly, at which it was amongst his daily duties to decant the stuff?

Anyway, he said that in the latter stages of his employ-ment he could count on average take-home pay of £27 per week, which would be the equivalent of £200 in today's debased currency: a fortune considering it was tax-free and pure pocket-money.

But money did not interest him, except from an intellectual point of view. He was completely unmercenary, although he loved to spin dubious yarns of how far a pound had stretched in his salad days – purchasing two seats at a music hall, programmes, chocolates during the show, ice-creams in the intervals, a four-course dinner and a bus-ride to the home of the piece of fluff who was ready for anything by that time. Where money was concerned, he acted as if he believed the Lord of lords would provide; and the strange thing was that the Lord did so, in spite of all Brownie's blaspheming.

The destination of most of his companions after a night out was the Piccadilly itself, which employed staff of both sexes. Maids cleaned the place and worked in the kitchens and, if they were single, also lived in. They were strictly supervised by an older housekeeper, and their rooms on the upper floors were sealed off from those of the lusty pages and waiters. Romance flourished nonetheless. Propinquity and sufficient opportunity performed their customary function. Brownie recalled not only formal evenings in theatres with girls who at any rate began by being on their best behaviour, but more earthy episodes on a dark stairway and behind an accessible chimneystack.

Round about the age of twenty-two he took a particular fancy to a pair of sisters with jobs at the club, Mary and Jenny.

Jenny was his favourite.

He married Mary.

*

Brownie's marital home was a flat he rented in Fulham.

Now he was a married man he was allowed occasional weekends off. On the Saturday morning of such a weekend he and his wife would go to see the sights at the Caledonian or Portobello markets. At length they would buy a whole branch of bananas – a hand of bananas, he called it. They returned to their flat and went to bed and stayed there until the Monday, just reaching out for a banana whenever they felt hungry.

The scene of the two of them in bed for nearly forty-eight hours, eating bananas and the rest of it, suggests happiness.

The fact remains that the monotony of marriage cannot have suited Brownie's temperament. Variety was much more than the spice of his life: variety was its very bread and

17

butter. Without change, excitement, challenges, and crisis and drama, which most people hope to get away from by marrying, he fell into a bored torpid state.

He was extraordinarily attractive to women of every sort, condition, age and class, notwithstanding his appearance, which struck other men as being on the unprepossessing side. Hereward once annoyed a vain Don Juan of his acquaintance by declaring that the greatest success with women he had ever known was Brownie.

And Hereward was simply telling the truth, not teasing.

Brownie was expert at charming, pleasing, surprising, interesting, engaging the sympathies of women and, above all, making them laugh. He seduced them physically or morally by means of the eternal infallible technique: tickling them.

Yet his attitude was ambivalent. Like rough boys, he scorned their frailties. He subscribed to jeering music hall opinions of pretty little dolly-birds, wives and mothers-in-law. He seemed to feel he was a battle-scarred veteran of the sex-war as well as the class-war, who must never yield or retreat.

The worst of it was that he came up against an extreme form of a common male difficulty. He could love but not live with women, generally speaking. Or, rather, he could and did win their love and attachment – and dull attachment was the last thing in the world he wanted. He aroused expectations which he had neither the intention nor the ability to fulfil.

Again and again he put himself in false positions that turned out to be untenable. He spoilt his women. He was such fun to be with, he pulled their legs, he gave them presents, he promised the moon, he was their slave. When he disappointed the hopes he had raised, he could not abide their shrill demands and reproaches – his nerves were not good enough.

Women were the chief representatives of that authority he was always opposed to. Drinking might have been an expression of the mutinous sentiments they inspired. It was easier to drink and forget than to tell a furious female he could not and would not and did not and was at the end of his amorous tether. Probably in pubs he recovered his sense of identity as a sex-war soldier together with other soldiers, refreshing themselves before slogging back into action against their fair and foul enemy.

That he should have married the wrong sister was typical. Setting aside his future causes of complaint, the women he was involved with were invariably wrong in one way or another – and subject to his critical ridicule and unflattering comparisons with men. He liked his liberty too much to be bothered with attempts at rectification. And it is perfectly possible that he let Mary lead him to the altar merely to oblige, when he wished to wed Jenny or not at all.

His conduct in 1939 tends to corroborate the notion that he had at least had his fill of nuptial bliss – by then he had been married for a year or two. He enlisted in the army before hostilities commenced. He was patriotic, he said – and why wait until he was called up? He persuaded the military doctors to pass him fit despite his hundred and fifty tumours.

Far be it from me to cast aspersions on his convictions and his courage.

At the same time his biographer is entitled to try to get to the bottom of his ambiguity.

He need not have been in such a hurry to enlist. He could have persuaded the doctors he was not a hundred per cent fit – he did in different circumstances. As it was he pauperised his wife unnecessarily soon, for a private in the army was then paid only a few shillings a week. The evidence is capable of the interpretation that what he could not wait for was escape from matrimony.

He volunteered for service in a Scottish regiment.

'I told them I was half a Scot through my mother.'

No doubt he omitted to add that his father had been Austrian.

2

Brownie's recollections of his years in the army were a trenchant comment on the confusion and absurdity of war.

Whether or not he ever told the whole true story is debatable. I suppose that as usual he himself, not really the war, was responsible for most of the confusion.

His ambition to get into a Scottish regiment was realised. After spending a few weeks with the Highland Light Infantry, he transferred into the Black Watch. He was prouder of having served in the Black Watch than of any of his other achievements. He felt it was a social distinction. The regimental tradition of toughness was right up his street.

He was stationed at barracks in Edinburgh and Glasgow: Auld Reekie and Glasgie, he called them in his travesty of a Scottish brogue. He would emphasise the nordic cold of the parade grounds on which he learnt to drill the Black Watch way: 'It was so cold a man's hands froze to the barrel of his rifle.' But some of his drilling must have been done in or near cities in Southern England with their kinder climate, Bath in Somerset and Lewes in Sussex, for instance, which he knew well.

He wore a kilt and sporran and nothing underneath.

He readily expatiated on – and must have exaggerated – the Black Watch attitude to nether garments.

'Wearing pants under a kilt was forbidden . . . Before leaving barracks, we had to prove we were properly dressed or undressed to the NCO on duty in the guard-room – showing a leg wasn't in it . . . We weren't allowed to travel on the upper deck of a bus, because of climbing the stairs . . . We could only get permission to wear pants if we were going in for Scottish dancing in mixed company . . . One sergeant-major of ours had a mirror fixed to the end of his yard-stick, so he could peep under our kilts to check that none of us had pants on . . . Another sergeant would give the command : 'Battalion, sit down !' – when snow was thick on the ground. Any man who was able to sit in the snow without moaning and groaning was placed in close arrest.'

Brownie at once complained of cold weather such as he experienced in the army and elsewhere, referring back to its dire effects on a Scottish soldier's unprotected parts, and boasted of the circulation of his blood.

'I'm centrally heated – my blood's always on the boil – I have to sleep on top of my blankets with the windows wide in mid-winter – and on summer nights you could fry an egg on me!'

He was pleased to remember that he had become as tough as his comrades in arms – and in years to come to think he remained so. He described forty-mile route-marches across the Cairngorms, carrying a full load of equipment, and other tests of strength and endurance he had passed. Being a Sassenach amongst Scotsmen – although he might have argued that point – and Cockney and an ex-waiter with von Recklinghausen's Disease, obviously put him on his mettle. In his free time he joined in brawls and pitched battles with Canadian troops : 'We threw Canadians through shop windows.' He kept on winning a corporal's stripe and losing it for having taken part in some act of hooliganism, more than likely

22

committed under the influence of alcohol – notwithstanding his far-fetched assertion that he was teetotal until after the war.

'We were savages – the local people were far more frightened of us than they were of the Germans,' he would say complacently.

He affected to despise the rest of the British army, not to mention the armies of our gallant allies.

With his future boss, who had been in the Royal Horse Guards, he indulged in competitive badinage.

'All the Brigade of Guards could do was spit and polish . . . Do you know our name for the Household Cavalry? We called them Piccadilly Cowboys . . . They did most of their parading behind the trees in Hyde Park after dark – with men in mackintoshes giving the orders . . . We were a fighting regiment!'

But then he let Hereward in on a secret cause of Black Watch embarrassment. A platoon was posted to guard a remote island in the Orkneys, where, it was later discovered, the men interfered with the sheep. They had wound their puttees round the beasts' legs to stop them running away, Brownie explained.

Thereafter his jibes at Hereward's expense could be countered by the single syllable: 'Baa!'

And Hereward would enquire: 'Who were the Black Watch fighting in the Orkneys? Have you heard the rumour that the sheep up there are giving birth to tartan lambs with built-in sporrans?'

Brownie had to laugh. The story amused more than it ever embarrassed him personally – and he was not averse to its publication. For it lent support to his mythology in respect of the licensed gang of roistering ruffians to which he once belonged, indiscriminately randy, lawless, afraid of nothing, belligerent and jealous of their reputation.

'We never retreated . . . We never shone our boots like your lot, we dubbined them, ready for active service . . . When the Guards saw the whites of the enemy's eyes, they sent for the Black Watch . . . The Germans meant it when they said we were devils-in-skirts!'

He played down the fact that owing to his qualifications he was soon in action in the Officers' Mess.

*

Meanwhile his daughter Peggy had been born.

His wife was all right for money, she had a well-paid job in a factory, and generously subsidised him when he was home on leave.

He waited on the Black Watch officers, picking up tips and compliments and contrarily preferring the authoritarians, just as he had at the Piccadilly Club, until his regiment was shipped over to France with the British Expeditionary Force.

Before long he was involved in the retreat to Dunkirk.

He made much of his war-wound. 'I shed my blood for king and country . . .' He was inclined to limp and confide in strangers that he did so because of the injuries he had sustained in battle.

Eventually, in response to Hereward's curious questioning, he provided a reasonably convincing answer.

'We were on the run,' he related.

Would he have admitted the Black Watch had retreated if he was not telling the truth? But you never knew with Brownie. He might have borrowed the whole scenario from a film.

24

'We were on the run,' he said. 'We were separated from our regiment – about a dozen of us with rifles and not even a Bren-gun. We were sheltering in the ruin of a cottage in the country, completely isolated – no other buildings nearby. An officer came roaring up in a Jeep and ordered us to gather round. He pointed to the landscape in front, a few flat fields in the shape of a wedge with woods on either side. He told us: "You see the gap between the trees? Any minute a Panzer Division with tanks is going to start rolling through it. You're to stop that Division – do you understand? You're staying here to fight to the last man and give the regiment a chance to retire to a more strategic position. And good luck to you!" Well – the officer buzzed off. We were left standing in full view of the blasted gap. We scuttled back into our cottage pretty damn quick. Of course we were scared – a dozen rifle-men against a Tank Division. My mates kept on pushing me forwards into the doorway to keep a look-out. I heard the report of a rifle and felt as if I'd been stung by a wasp or a bee. When something warm started trickling down my legs I thought I must have disgraced myself – that was how scared we all were. But suddenly I noticed my boots were full of blood. The next thing I knew was that I'd been taken prisoner.'

'Had you been stung by a bee or had you been shot?'

'Shot, sir.'

'Whereabouts?'

'In the leg, sir.'

'If you were shot in one leg, why did blood trickle down both of them and into both your boots?'

'I was shot in the thigh, sir, and high up the thigh at that.'

'You mean you were shot in the posterior?'

'More in the hip, please, sir. The bullet just missed my vitals.'

25

'How lucky for you!'

'You can say that again – if it's luck to be seriously wounded and a prisoner of war for a hell of a long time.'

'I'm sorry, Brownie – don't think me unsympathetic – I was concentrating on your vitals, which you were lucky to hang on to. But I want to try to get the picture straight. What happened between your being shot and being captured?'

'I passed out, sir.'

'Fainted, you mean?'

'No, sir. I lost consciousness because my life-blood was draining into my boots.'

'Did you come to in hospital?'

'The Germans treated me in one of their hospitals. But I had to do a tremendous march before I was anywhere near a hospital.'

'So you were able to march although you were seriously wounded?'

'There was no alternative, sir.'

'Were you still bleeding as you marched?'

'Not all the way, sir. I clenched the wound together with my hand.'

'Really? What sort of a wound was it?'

'A sort of deep graze.'

'Only a graze?'

'A sort of very deep painful graze.'

'I see. What became of that Panzer Division? Did it get through?'

'We couldn't stop it, sir. I was knocked out. My mates were captured along with me. Most of the Black Watch Battalion was caught in the bag.'

'And you tottered into Germany with your hand on your hip?'

'Beg pardon, sir – I wasn't ever in the Household Cavalry.'

26

On numerous occasions Hereward and Brownie resumed their droll duelling over the latter's experiences as a casualty and prisoner of war.

'Who shot you?'

'It was the Germans, sir.'

'You sound a trifle doubtful.'

'No, sir. Why should I be?'

'Well – you said the Germans were in front of your ruined cottage. The Panzer Division was on the point of advancing through a gap between two woods in front. And you were shot in the rear.'

'It was a ricochet, sir.'

'Are you quite sure you weren't shot by a friend or a foe of yours in the Black Watch? You said you were pushed forward into the doorway by the other fellows. Maybe somebody wanted a bit of space to take aim and plug you.'

'Never, sir! A trigger could have been pulled accidentally, because everyone was so dithery. But that's a different matter.'

'I agree. And don't get me wrong. But haven't you often told me old scores were settled and unpopular officers and men were polished off by their own side in the heat of battle?'

'I might have done.'

'How unpopular were you?'

'I was the original forces' favourite.'

On another tack Hereward enquired: 'Listen, Brownie – honestly – how was it you came to be shot in that particular part of your anatomy? You say you were facing the Germans in your doorway. Isn't the exact reverse closer to the truth?'

'The Black Watch never turns its back on the enemy, sir.'

'But you've confessed you were on the run.'

'We were running for cover to fight from.'

'Did you know that in some regiments a wound such as

27

yours is considered to be conclusive proof of cowardice and grounds for a court-martial?'

'I know that if I'd been in the American army I would have got the Purple Heart.'

'Do you think you deserved a medal?'

'Definitely I should have got the Purple Something-or-other for what I suffered and where I suffered it.'

His sufferings included starving in a POW camp.

'I used to dream of babies' heads and two veg.' – babies' heads were the steak and kidney puddings obtainable in that pub behind the Piccadilly Club.

'Was it awful, Brownie?'

'It was until I was taken to hospital.'

'To have your wound dressed?'

'Yes, sir.'

'Weren't you taken to hospital immediately?'

'Not soon enough. The German doctors were more interested in my tumours than my wound. I'm a medical freak, you see.'

'Are you telling me you got to hospital because of your tumours – and your bleeding bottom never needed attention?'

'In a manner of speaking.'

'But I understood your wound was so serious?'

'That's right, sir – or it would have been if I wasn't a rapid healer. I heal as quick as an animal, probably on account of the gipsy in me.'

'Well – anyway – were the doctors kind to you?'

'Oh yes, sir. The Germans are a marvellous race. I never had any quarrel with the Germans. One of their doctors asked me to be his batman.'

'What did you say?'

'Yes, sir.'

'What?'

28

'It was better being his batman than mooching round the camp with nowt to eat.'

'But he was an enemy – you were betraying your country by co-operating with the enemy.'

'He was more of a gentleman than many I've worked for over here. And I'm half-Austrian, remember.'

'For heaven's sake, Brownie – did you join the German army in the middle of the war? Which side were you on? I'm getting in more and more of a muddle.'

'What's muddling? I did what I could to keep body and soul together. And I was only working for my doctor for a shortish spell. He issued me with a certificate of invalidity and then I was repatriated.'

'Sent home?'

'Yes, sir.'

'Because of your tumours again?'

'Exactly.'

'How long did you spend in the POW camp?'

'Six or seven months.'

'Six months! That's not a hell of a long time. My impression was that you were there for the duration. I've been feeling sorry for you for having been imprisoned for years!'

'It seemed like years, sir.'

*

Brownie added: 'Besides, I was recaptured and locked up in another POW camp before the war ended.'

The indubitable fact that he once more persuaded the British doctors to pass him fit to fight, when the Germans had come to the conclusion he was so unfit as to constitute no further danger or threat to themselves, was extra evidence

29

of his courage – and the reason why Hereward felt free in a humorous context to call it in question.

He was re-trained by the Black Watch. He returned to France soon after D-day.

'I was part of the Allied Forces' spearhead.'

'Brownie – we know you were shot and wounded – did you ever shoot anybody?'

'Yes, sir.'

'How many of the enemy did you knock out?'

'One, sir.'

'No more than one?'

'And he was a mile off. But I got him in my rifle-sights and let the poor basket have it.'

'What makes you think you hit him?'

'He jumped in the air and rolled over like a rabbit.'

Brownie's second Stalag was worse than the first: 'We had to work on the land – the Germans were short of food – and we were so hungry we ate raw turnips in the fields.'

But he adapted to circumstances as usual.

The polite version of how he did so ran as follows: 'I was detailed to work on a smallholding that belonged to an old Prussian farmer and his wife. I helped to look after everything on the smallholding, especially the pigs. They're beautiful creatures, pigs, and much cleaner than human beings. If I have to come back to earth in the shape of an animal when I die, I'd like to be a pig. The farmer and his wife were all over me, they were grateful, and gave me food, an egg or two and now and then a slice of bacon, which I smuggled into camp in my glengarry and shared with the lads.' His glengarry was the Scottish cap worn by the Black Watch. 'I kept quite a few of the lads going with the victuals I slipped them.'

The impolite version was less altruistic and more likely.

'The farmer was past it – he was about seventy. His wife

Olga was thirty and a great blonde buxom thing. It was harvest-time when I started working for them – we were busy until late at night and again at the crack of dawn. They asked for permission to let me sleep in their house, which was really more of a shack – just a kitchen and a room above; and I promised not to try to escape and was granted parole. I thought I'd be sleeping in the kitchen. But on the first evening the farmer took my hand and led me upstairs and pointed to the double bed in the bedroom. We climbed into it together. Again I thought he wanted to check on my movements and stop me escaping. But he stayed on his side of the bed and began to snore – and Olga was in the middle. Of course it was ding-dong the whole night through. And afterwards Olga couldn't have enough. She even got at me in the pigsty. The most peculiar part was that the farmer was more grateful to me than ever for making his young wife happy. He used to say: "Brown do Olga good" – which was a funny way of putting it, considering. "Ja, ja, mein Herr – Brown done Olga good a couple of times today," I shouted back at him. And he laughed and patted my cheek – and she gave me another plateful of meat dumplings and sauerkraut. That Olga, she fed me like a fighting cock – none of your naughty comments, please, sir. She and her hubby were dead-keen on keeping my strength up. The fellows in camp couldn't understand why I got fatter and fatter while they were skin and bones.'

'Didn't you explain why?'

'No, sir – still tongue, wise head, as the saying goes.' He would tap his square forehead and declare: 'Five hundred thousand brain-cells in here and none of them filled with beeswax.' He often had recourse to a similar canny dictum: 'There are no flies on me – only the marks where they have been.'

'But didn't you smuggle any titbits from the smallholding into camp?'

'I couldn't smuggle meat dumplings and gravy in my glengarry, sir.'

'Didn't you smuggle anything? I've heard you telling people you provided your friends with victuals. Was that a lie?'

'No, sir. I'm no *proverber* of the truth.' He meant perverter. 'I'd smuggle an egg or a scrap of bacon when I remembered to. But I needed all the nourishment I could get, working day and night as I was.'

'And mostly flat out.'

'Thank you, sir. My friends wouldn't have smuggled and run risks and denied themselves to share their buckshee rations with me – they weren't stupid. And my religion was against it.'

'What religion?'

'The first and last commandment of my religion wouldn't have let me act any different.'

'What's that, Brownie?'

'Take care of number one.'

*

It was his biggest lie that he took care of number one.

He repeated and even seemed to believe that he was motivated by exclusive self-interest. In reality and on the contrary, his life was spent in taking care of others. In the midst of war, in prison camps, he found someone to take care of, for instance his German doctor, and again in a sense Olga and her complaisant husband and their pigs. His chief ambition was to please and indeed increase the sum of

32

happiness in the world; and in order to fulfil it he was always prepared to renounce his ego.

At the same time it has to be admitted that he generally did what he wanted to do, what made him happy, and that he was infinitely crafty at turning every situation to his own advantage and far from blind to the main chance. He pleased – which pleased him – and as a rule he was rewarded for pleasing sooner or later. He was at once as patient as Job, and the person in the Chinese adage to whom all things come because they have been waited for.

He was either sensible and down to earth and practical, or cynical, depending on the angle from which he was observed. He would not shed a tear for his fellow-prisoners while he demolished Olga's dinners; how was he to appease their communal hunger? Why should he as well as they go hungry?

Moreover he lived for the moment. The gratification of Olga was his immediate concern and best bet. His inclinations, natural, physical and politic, obliged him to do justice to her cooking. Pointless qualms of conscience would have spoilt his appetite.

Hereward agreed that Brownie might be destined for heaven – but with reservations.

'He won't sneak past the pearly gates until he's explained to St Peter how it was that he fell on his feet over and over again, when his friends were falling on their heads.'

Hereward could have mentioned Brownie's use or abuse of religion for the sake of a joke – which was unlikely to endear him to St Peter.

'My God is punctuality,' he reiterated.

And he countered incredulity and scepticism by invoking and challenging the deity: 'Let the Lord God Almighty strike me dead as I stand here if I tell a lie!' – an oath not only foolhardy, but eventually counter-productive, since in the human ears of the initiated it was proof positive that the truth was being *proverbed*.

Anyway the war ended. His romantic story was that he was liberated by a young female Russian soldier, who leant a plank against the wire perimeter fence of the camp and rode in over the top.

He also claimed there was a concentration-camp in the area, where Jews had been incinerated: 'We sniffed them like Bisto Kids provided the wind was in the right direction.' Again the Russians liberated the surviving inmates. Brownie, notwithstanding his shocking pleasantries, was distressed by the dreadful sights he said he saw. Yet he continued to proclaim his admiration for the Germans – objectively, genuinely, provocatively, and partly for racialist reasons.

His attitude to other races betrayed his social origins. His conscious considered opinion was that he had risen above the working class and its prejudices. Even if he sometimes called himself a peasant or a serf, he would speak in terms as patronising as they were scathing of the idleness, greed, irresponsibility and folly of the British post-war worker. Whether or not a beneficial phenomenon of our class system is that nobody can believe he is the common man, Brownie was justifiably convinced that he was uncommon – 'when they made me they threw away the mould' – or had become so owing to his contacts with the gentry. And his socially superior persona had a special liking for individual Jews and Negroes – he sympathised with their minority plight, told them he was a gipsy, teased them outrageously, and often established relations of mutual trust and affection. But in the event of trouble, in Jewish shops for instance, or when he caught sight of blacks queueing to draw the dole from a Social

34

Security office, he cursed the races they belonged to. Instinctively and ineradicably he reverted to subscribing to the worst fear of poor people everywhere: namely of strangers muscling in on their scant preserves.

After peace broke out, and before he was demobilised, he transferred into the Military Police. The various roles he played between 1939 and 1946 – Highland Light Infantryman, Black Watchman, fighting man, Officers' Mess orderly, prisoner, German doctor's servant, invalid, pig-fancier, and finally, as he impressed simpletons by abbreviating it, M.P. – were more like transformations in a pantomime than official transfers or anything else. He remained in Germany, his principal task being to trace contraband which had been stolen from army stores for sale on the black market.

He must have excelled at it. He had a native genius for concealment – and developed it when he began to drink too much – so was in the position of poacher turned gamekeeper. In the same way that he loved to hide things and secretively cover his tracks, he loved to seek.

I can imagine him on the job: padding round the premises of suspected black marketeers, quieter than usual, his slightly bulbous eyes missing nothing, terrifyingly perspicacious. Once, he related, he and a colleague ransacked a flat in vain. They had examined every room in the place thoroughly and unsuccessfully. As they were leaving Brownie hurried back to the bathroom: the wife of the proprietor had been having a deep bath there. He pulled out the bath-plug. She was lying naked on dozens of tins of Spam.

Discoveries of another sort were in store for him in Civvy Street. His marriage was on the rocks, although he – or she – still hoped to salvage it. The problems of the Browns were typical of the times: they had been married for seven or eight years and only together for one or two.

35

What might have been more tragic for Brownie was the rejection of his application to resume work at the Piccadilly Club. Apparently he was told by a secretary that the club was now staffed by immigrant Italians, his former enemies.

3

His repudiation by the Piccadilly was cruel – and cinematic. It seems too neatly ironical, his job being filched by members of a race he had fought against, and that he should thus be penalised for his patriotism. It is improbable on several counts: the club authorities would have been crazy not to jump at the chance of re-employing him. For that matter would he have wanted to work anti-social hours in London, when he was living with his wife and daughter in Kent and doing his utmost to preserve his marriage?

The Piccadilly no longer exists. Brownie has covered his tracks.

He signed on at a Royal Doulton factory.

'Were you making lavatories?'

'No, sir – bone china!'

He then switched into the construction industry. He was engaged in building the West Kent Power Station. He worked as a labourer on one of the tall chimneys, some hundreds of feet above the ground. He was well paid and received extra danger-money. But he was always short of cash, because of the gambling on site.

'The men played cards and gambled all the time, even on the scaffold, and expected me to join in. They were a rough

37

crew – you had to be rough to put up with the conditions in winter.'

West Kent Power Station is in the vicinity of the Thames Estuary. Almost throughout the year icy winds from the sea swayed the scaffolding alarmingly; and mud and wet cement on boots rendered the rungs of ladders and the catwalks of planking slippery; and hands were so chilled that they could not grip the poles. One day a fellow missed his footing and fell to his death.

'How did you react?'

'Badly, sir.'

'Well – no wonder.'

'I thanked God it wasn't Brownie – and stayed where I was, clinging on at the top, until they'd cleared the mess away.'

A contributory cause of his shortage of cash may have been his expenditure on liquid refreshment. No doubt the post-war hour had struck at which – he would admit – he had started drinking or drinking in earnest. He said that at the Power Station it was difficult not to.

'The best men on the scaffold swigged a quart of beer first thing in the morning. They just poured it down their throats – they wouldn't venture near a ladder without it. The beer relaxed their muscles. Otherwise they would have been too tense and jittery.'

'Did you follow their example?'

'Yes, sir. That's why I'm here today. The teetotallers were turned into strawberry jam.'

Additional pressures were driving him to or towards drink. In spite of his adaptability he had had by no means a cushy war. He came home to find his marriage in pieces and, possibly, that he was superfluous to requirements at the Piccadilly. In factories and on scaffolding he was wasting his talents – he was something like a creative artist denying his art and growing destructive or self-destructive in consequence. And he was not half as rough and tough as he pretended to be.

He was unhappy. He was drowning his sorrows. But he was never at a loss for such excuses. Life never failed to provide him with first-class excuses to overdo it as he pleased.

The pub became – or already was – the oasis in the desert of his existence. He knew by heart the name of every public house he had ever frequented: the way he rolled those names round his tongue evoked scenes of Dickensian brightness, warmth, jollity and good cheer. Pubs were his clubs, where he felt protected from the outside world of demanding women and authority; where with the help of a little of what he fancied – or a lot – he could shed his cares; where he chewed the rag and shot a line, and formed the sort of temporary friendships he preferred, which posed no threat to his privacy. For pubs were also the stages on which he performed semi-professionally, entertaining, imitating his bosses, clowning – he was not keen on members of his audience prying behind the scenes.

His troubles multiplied, perhaps not only as troubles are inclined to, but as they invariably did when he was in the grip of the demon.

Against his will he had been forced to join a Trade Union. He disapproved of Union methods, the intimidation and the blackmail, and eventually tore up his Membership Card at a public meeting. Then he had a fall from the scaffolding. He was lucky enough to land on a horizontal pole ten feet below and save himself; but he lost his nerve and his head for heights. The result was that he either resigned his job or was kicked out of it by Union officialdom.

Meanwhile Mrs Brown was dividing her time between her husband and the man she had lived with during the war:

again I am quoting Brownie. Increasingly violent quarrels ensued – and crimes were committed that gave ample scope for unpleasantness in the future.

He had to scrounge the wherewithal to keep at any rate two bodies and souls together, his own and his daughter Peggy's. He had an allotment where he grew vegetables, a bicycle and a mongrel called Lassie. He was very fond of Lassie: she used to run along the street and leap into his arms when he rode home on his bicycle. One fine day Mrs Brown had the dog put down.

'For no reason?'

'No proper reason, sir.'

'Was nothing wrong with her?'

'She was three years old and in the pink, although my wife wouldn't have it.'

'You mean your wife said that Lassie was ill?'

'She said so. And she procured a certificate from the vet. But I know she did it to spite me.'

'I suppose you had your revenge?'

'Oh yes, sir. Nobody gets away with twisting my tail.'

A suspect feature of the story of Lassie was the mournful relish with which Brownie repeated it, in order to enlist sympathy, whenever the collapse of his marriage was mentioned. He added embellishments to wring the hearts of his listeners: no dog had ever been so obedient and faithful as his Lass.

But whether or not Mrs Brown really carried her spite to lethal extremes, she must have been provoked by her spouse's customary response to stress. He was poor and unhappy, therefore he squandered money in pubs and made himself miserable: that was his paradoxical theory – or habitual practice. He was under the common illusion of drinking people: he imagined a few drinks did him a power of good, sharpened his wits, enabled him to cope, whereas in fact they simply stupefied him.

And their after-effects in his case were psychologically as well as physically damaging. He suffered from guilt. Guilt and shame between them induced a passive masochistic state, which tempted the opposite sex in particular to vent its spleen on him. His boldness with women when he was sober emboldened them when he was or had been drunk : often they seemed to visit on his unprotesting person the accumulated bitterness of all their defeats in the war with men. To keep them quiet, and as penance, he renewed the solemn extravagant promises he could not and would not honour. He was again reproached, he had a few more drinks, he sank back into his infuriating lethargy, he asked for another dose of punishment, and the vicious circle was complete.

The upshot of this murky period of Brownie's life – unemployed, at odds with and more or less separated from his wife who was not kind to him, penniless, dogless, and probably half seas over – was that he decided to look for the type of work he was best at in London.

In 1950 he may indeed have applied in vain for his old job at the Piccadilly : by that time the club was in financial straits and its exclusive policy could have been to employ cheap Italian labour.

He managed to trace the club's pre-war hall-porter, who was now a commissionaire at a luxury hotel. He explained his predicament to Mr Triggs and said he was ready to go into private service. Should Mr Triggs hear of any decent situation, would he let Brownie know ?

*

Soon afterwards Hereward Watkins began to play his part in Brownie's destiny, and vice versa.

Hereward was then aged twenty-three, while Brownie was in his mid-thirties.

Hereward had served his term in the Household Cavalry and been demobilised, wanted to write and was eager to apprentice himself to literature. But he was hard up, notwithstanding his well-to-do family and Watkins Hall in the Brecon Beacons. A married sister vacated her flat in the West End of London and suggested that he should take it and move in. Although he agreed he would work better there than in the spare rooms of hospitable friends, he said it was way beyond his means.

The flat was a maisonette on the two top floors of a large house in Windle Road, just north of Oxford Street. The place was owned and the rest of it occupied by a learned society, the Antipodean Archaeological Trust, which was disposed to lease its residential accommodation for a minimal rent to a recommended tenant.

Hereward had second thoughts. The maisonette was a bargain and thanks to his sister he was in a position to obtain the lease. Granted, minimal as the rent was, he could not afford it. On the other hand he might be able to sub-let the three rooms and bathroom on the lower floor.

By chance he met a Frenchman, Jacques Beausson, who was in a hurry to find somewhere to live. Jacques was a prosperous banker, thirty or so, and working in the English branch of his bank. He needed a good accessible address, since he had to wine and dine business contacts in the evenings, and room for a servant who would cook for and generally look after him.

He approved of the maisonette on being shown round it. His servant could have one of the rooms on the upper floor, leaving Hereward with two, which would do him nicely. The financial details were sorted out to their mutual satisfaction. Hereward felt it was worth investing most of his capital in the necessary furnishings.

Temporarily Jacques happened to be staying in the hotel where Mr Triggs was the commissionaire.

On the appointed day he therefore arrived at Windle Road with Brownie in tow.

At first Hereward did not take to him. And he was none too sure that he liked the idea of having to share his new home with a foreign acquaintance and a total stranger. But in time he changed his mind.

Jacques was not a typical Frenchman: he was taciturn and reserved. He worked hard, left for his office early and returned late, stayed with English friends at weekends and travelled abroad on business a good deal. He was careful not to impose upon or bother Hereward, and kept strictly to his own floor of the maisonette. His discretion was appreciated, while his contribution to expenses relieved Hereward of money worries. In addition Jacques was literary, respected Hereward's endeavours in that line, and his initial trials and errors, and encouraged him to persevere with the novels that eventually made his name.

Brownie – or Brown as he was called to begin with – struck Hereward as too obsequious.

My memory tells me I was present at their meeting. It was long ago – but I seem to remember climbing the stairs to Hereward's quarters and being greeted by a short smiling man with flat sandy-coloured hair brushed back and parted in the middle: he had emerged from the kitchen on to the top landing. Jacques, who was not present, must have admitted him to the maisonette and left him to his own devices – and perhaps I had been having lunch somewhere with

43

Hereward preparatory to lending a hand with his unpacking.

'How do you do, sir – Brown, sir!'

He was standing to attention. He barked his name and the sirs. But he shook hands and smiled with a certain charm. He was thin in those days – thin, active, quick, lively, like a terrier. I noticed his broad face and square forehead and popping blue eyes. He wore a black bow-tie and white waiter's jacket.

'Is everything all right, Brown?'

'Yes, sir, thank you, sir. Would you like to inspect my room, sir?'

He led us into it. His shaving tackle was laid out with extraordinary precision on the shelf above the washbasin. A framed snapshot of his daughter was exactly in the centre of the bedside table. His blankets had been folded and piled with scrupulous neatness at the foot of the bed.

'You must have been in the army.'

'Six years and four months in the Black Watch, sir!'

'Really? Are you Scottish?'

'Half-Scottish, sir – my mother was a Macgregor.'

'Obviously you haven't forgotten your army training.'

'I was always regimental, sir.' By regimental he meant tidy. 'Is there anything I can do for you, sir?'

'Oh – no. No, thanks. Well, I'll see you later, Brown.'

Hereward expressed his doubts as soon as he and I were alone.

'I don't fancy that three-bags-full approach. I've never in my life been called sir so often in such a short space of time. He's too good to be true – he's smarmy. Anyway he's Jacques' servant, not mine. I know he's got glowing references, but I couldn't bear to have him dancing attendance on me.'

At four or five o'clock on the same afternoon, as I recollect it, there was a knock on the door of Hereward's sitting-room.

'Yes? Who is it? Come in!'

'Beg pardon, sir – I wondered if I could bring you a nice tray of tea?'

'How thoughtful of you, Brown. As a rule I don't stop for tea. I may fetch a cup in a little while. But don't you trouble yourself.'

'It's no trouble, sir. I've already laid the tray for two. Indian or China, sir?'

'Have you got both sorts?'

'Yes, sir – I've just been to the shops.'

'Well, in that case, China, please.'

'And some hot buttered toast with strawberry jam, sir?'

'What about Monsieur Beausson? Where's Monsieur Beausson? Won't he be wanting tea?'

'He said he'd only dash in to change his clothes this evening, sir.'

'Well – if you're sure it isn't too much trouble, maybe we will have toast and jam.'

'Thank you, sir.'

'No – thank you, Brown.'

Brownie was on his very best behaviour. He was out to prove he was not too good to be true. He was practising the seductive art of his dance of attendance. And his gratitude was sincere inasmuch as he was pleased to be given the opportunity to please.

But he was also acting a part – and with such expertise that neither Hereward nor I, although we had both been in the army, realised quite how much of his obsequious manner would have been called bullshit in a barrack-room.

Again, Londoners as we were, even if Hereward hailed from Wales, we failed to recognise in him that traditionally

45

Cockney phenomenon of a person for whom every single aspect of existence is a potential joke.

We were slow in the uptake. It was some years before we got the point.

Jacques never got it. French people may be wittier than the English; they cannot be as relentlessly, broadly, inclusively humorous as Brownie, who was after all unique. Temperamental or national misunderstandings between employer and employee at Windle Road were to blame for future discord.

I must not anticipate.

The fanciful sequel to our first encounter that I visualise with hindsight is Brownie in some pub, holding forth over a frothing tankard and making mock of Hereward's efforts not to exploit him: 'I hadn't been in the house two minutes before my boss starts pressing the bell. That's what they think their fingers are for – pressing bells for flunkeys. Bring me tea and a stack of hot toast spread thick with best butter, he says. And he wouldn't touch the tea you and I drink, matey – not he. His tea's flown in fresh from China every day – I had to walk two miles to Fortnum and Mason and back again to buy it. The habits of the upper crust are peculiar, believe me! Mr Hereward Watkins, the Earl of Grimlingham, Graf von Twisch, Lord Tatters Tatham – I've known the lot. I could tell you stories about them that would make your hair stand on end.'

*

I often spent Sundays with Hereward. We would meet for lunch after each of us had done five or six hours' writing, then go for a long walk and probably to a movie, and have an evening meal and part at the nearest bus-stop. Occasionally

46

other friends joined us. They were hard up, too, and impatient to hear what it was like to have a manservant at your beck and call.

Hereward satisfied our curiosity. He was equally intrigued by Brownie, whom he was beginning to appreciate. He in his turn was grateful for the opportunity to get on with his work without having to waste time on practicalities.

Officially Brownie was free to visit his family at weekends. But he was inclined to stay put in London – to save himself the expense of travelling to Kent, or because of his strained relations with his wife, or because he was afraid of yielding to alcoholic temptation on his home ground. In the early days at Windle Road he was either not drinking much, or his drinking had not attracted anyone's attention : a new job and new faces were exciting enough to keep him happy – and pretty sober.

On Sundays when he was in residence he would beg Hereward to let him do the catering. A card-table was erected in the little sitting-room on the top floor, and Hereward and I and any extra guests were duly fed and waited on. They had a special piquancy, those feasts served in princely style to our group of needy and even hungry aspirants for fame and fortune.

It was on Brownie's Sundays in London that I began to talk and listen to him, and mainly eavesdrop on the amusing serial of his dialogue with Hereward.

In passing, in defence of Hereward, I should explain that Brownie's offers of supererogatory service were only accepted in Jacques' absence. Hereward was always loath to seem to be taking the slightest advantage of his tenant's servant. And he was considerate, whatever the imaginative slander that may have been spread around in the local hostelries.

Apparently Jacques was aware of how difficult it was to

stop Brownie acting out his role and had no objection to his being kept occupied. He was the opposite of a dog in the manger – he was delighted to think of Hereward enjoying the manger's contents when he could not. A side-effect of his generous attitude and his absenteeism was that up to a point Brownie came to regard Hereward as his boss, while Hereward was drawn into assuming more and more of a boss's responsibilities and obligations – which were later on to form his payment in full for all benefits received.

But again I must not anticipate.

Jacques' prime concern was that Brownie should learn to cook. He was satisfied with his dispositions at Windle Road except in that respect. He appealed for advice to the hotel – and its commissionaire Mr Triggs – where he had stayed on arriving in England. Consequently Brownie spent a few weeks studying in the hotel's kitchens.

He proved an apt pupil. Cooking expressed the artistic part of his nature. Cooking could be said to be the art he had always sought. He loved the challenge of it, and the drama, the thrills and spills, and the implicit snobbery, and the competitive and boastful avenues it opened. He was greedy, he was neat-fingered, precise, inventive, intuitive, and presented food beautifully – presentation and the look of things counted for more with him than reality: he had most of the attributes of the best cooks. He never felt he was a hundred per cent alive unless he was frantically busy, sweating and cursing, for instance over a hot stove.

The chefs at the hotel were French. He acquired their lingo along with the tricks of their trade. And he could have been imitating Jacques, when he travestied the glottal stop. He now started to speak of por-h-ridge, o-h-ranges and so on.

'What would you like for lunch today, sir?'

'Oh – bangers and mash.'

'*Les sausages* and *pommes pur-h-ée*. And a green *salade*, sir?'

'Okay, Brownie.'

He was an out-and-out culinary name-dropper.

'Brownie, I can't think of anything to eat – my mind's a blank. Make a suggestion, will you?'

'Well, sir, you could have Chicken *Napoléon* with *petits pois* and *pommes fantastiques*, followed by *chocolat soufflé* or a cold *o-h-range mousse*.'

'What's Chicken Napoleon?'

'It was dreamt up by the chef of *Napoléon*, sir, during the reatreat from Moscow. All he had in his travelling larder was bread and butter and some *vin rouge*. The troops foraging in the countryside brought him a scrawny old fowl and a capful of *tomates*. He cooked his ingredients together in a pot over a camp fire and produced a very tasty dish. You should try it, sir.'

'How long does it take to prepare?'

'Five hours.'

'Five hours! But I only want a snack. What are *pommes fantastiques* anyway?'

'Balls, sir.'

'What did you say?'

'I said they're potato balls, sir. I scoop the balls from potatoes with my handy tool and roast them golden brown in the oven. They're like miniature crunchy *pommes rôtis*.'

'I see. But you misunderstood me, Brownie. I'm alone for supper and couldn't face a complicated meal – and I hate the idea of your slaving for hours on end to feed me.'

'Would you like a fresh *poisson*, sir, with *pommes allumettes*?'

'Do you mean fish and chips?'

'Yes, sir.'

49

'No. But I'll tell you what I would like: have you got a tin of sardines? Give me sardines and an apple, Brownie.'

'Very good, sir.'

The recipe for his Chicken *Napoléon* required dissection of the bird. He would illustrate the method of dissecting it on his own body.

'First you cut off its wings.' With his hand with fingers outstretched, simulating the blade of a knife, he would as it were carve from the side of his neck, down his chest and round and under his arm. 'Then you force its legs apart and cut them loose.' He would bend his knees and open his legs and carve from his groin up to his waist. 'And next you dig out its oysters.' He would turn and gesture graphically in the vicinity of the small of his back. 'If you need to separate the drum-sticks from the thighs you'll have to cut through here' – his hand sawed across his knee-joint.

He was liable to get his French wrong. He was taught to cook a savoury of ham and cheese fried between slices of bread, which is called *Croque Monsieur* in France. He called it *Coq Monsieur*. But maybe he meant to be rude. He had a lot of intentional fun with his description of *pommes fantastiques*.

His mistakes in English were also laughable, whether by accident or on purpose. He could not speak the word people except in the plural: 'I don't like a crowd of peoples.' He said Volga when he meant vulgar.

'No, Brownie – the Volga is the river where the boatmen sing.'

'Is it, sir? I thought I was Volga, and those boatmen were singing a vulgar song.'

Instead of 'a lick and a promise' he said 'a cat's lick and a promise': 'I've only given your room a cat's lick and a promise this morning.' Because of his fondness for pigs, or from

50

more ambiguous motives, he adapted the phrase cat's whiskers: 'You look like the pig's whiskers, sir!'

He said poonah for puma – 'as fierce as the poonahs in the zoo'; adolt for adult – 'he ought to know better at his age – after all he's an adolt'; charmed for chimed – 'the clock charmed six'; dappy for dapper – 'he was dappy in his brand new suit'; dole for doll – 'she's as pretty as a little dole'; hammer and tonk for hammer and tongs; Japanese scrawl for Japanese scroll; loveable for lovely – 'we had a loveable duck for dinner'; maulers for molars – 'I can eat the toughest meat with my maulers'; pendulum for pendant – 'Madame was wearing a great pendulum of diamonds'; and pus for pith – 'when you're making my sauce of *o-h-ranges*, you must be sure to use the pus – it's pus that adds the special flavour to my *o-h-range* sauce'.

*

His cooking improved out of recognition after his course at the hotel. Then Jacques invited a friend to stay in his spare room, Madame Drey, who gave Brownie extra lessons. Madame Drey was about sixty. She was a bad advertisement for her skills with food, being skeletally thin. She had a cigarette in her mouth and a glass in her hand for most of every day. But she and Brownie shut themselves into the kitchen at Windle Road. And she put the finishing touches to his education.

Jacques began to entertain his business contacts, as planned.

Brownie shopped for and prepared and carried downstairs and served and carried up the remains of mammoth meals, infinitely more complicated than the one he had suggested to Hereward.

'What was on the menu last night?'

'*Consommé* and *croûtons* to start with, and *sole vé-h-ronique* done in a white sauce with peeled grapes, and a sweet *gigot*, still pink inside just as Monsieur Beausson likes it, and *haricots* and oodles of my *pommes fantastiques*, and a *soufflé* of *chocolat*, and a board of *fromages* and a bowl of *fruit*.'

'Did they actually eat all that?'

'Not Monsieur Beausson – he's a very small eater. But the others did. I had to go round the table twice with my *gigot*. And they got through three French loaves as long as your arm and a pint of cream with the *soufflé* and their coffee.'

'They must have been hungry.'

'A gentleman told me he'd been starving himself all day so as to make room for my dinner.'

'What did they drink?'

'Chilled white wine with the fish, and *vin rouge* at room temperature with the meat, and brandy with the coffee. And they had gin and vodka before they sat down.'

'Did you serve the wine or was it passed round?'

'I served it, sir.'

'Isn't such a big dinner party a bit much for you?'

'Oh no, sir! I love it! I was like a wet flannel by the end of the evening – the sweat was pouring off me.'

'Over the guests?'

'They were past noticing by that time, sir.'

'Well – please tell me if you ever find the work too much – I'd try to explain to Monsieur Beausson.'

'I will, sir, thank you, sir. But I feel fit today – I could easily do it again.'

His duties, onerous as they were on festive occasions, did not seem so to him because they were still a novelty. He was buoyed up by being good at his job, and getting better, by compliments, and by his mystique of inexhaustible toughness. And he himself in his enthusiasm doubled those duties. He would plead with Jacques for permission to cook a chicken with tarragon, although tarragon was out of season and he knew he would really have to walk to Fortnum and Mason to buy it. He walked unnecessary miles and scoured Soho for recondite herbs and spices which he rather than Jacques insisted on using.

He had great respect for his employer, and affection and loyalty, at least on the surface. He was flattered to ascribe the highest standards to his Monsieur Beausson, and the most delicate palate. He was responsive to the trust reposed in him and sensed the gentleness and kindness underlying Jacques' somewhat impenetrable manner. He was impressed by the princes of industry and commerce who came to gorge themselves at Windle Road, and the foreign visitors who stayed in the spare room, Madame Drey, Colonel de Chiffre and the rest.

But the Cockney mentality with Celtic trimmings of fey-ness and fantasy, and the logical Latin one, are poles apart. When Jacques asked Brownie how many guests he could manage and received the boastful reply: 'The more the merrier, sir!' – he took Brownie literally. When Colonel de Chiffre asked for the name of a reputable laundry in the neighbourhood and was told not to worry – Brownie would be delighted to wash Monsieur le Colonel's shirts – the same thing happened. There was so much of the Celt in Brownie that his native tongue should have been Gaelic, which does not include any equivalent of the word no. As a result he assumed an ever increasing work-load.

And Jacques was too preoccupied to take note of the problem.

The fact was – as he saw it – that Brownie had more than

enough spare time in which to recuperate from dinner parties, despite his determined attendance on Hereward. He could go away for weekends if he chose to, and enjoyed completely free holiday spells while Jacques was travelling abroad and Hereward was down at Watkins Hall. He kept on saying the job suited him. He seemed to be settled and content.

His seeming contentment was always a danger signal. It could mean he was bored.

After he had been at Windle Road for about five years, his wife instituted proceedings for divorce and he had cause to console himself.

Or perhaps he started drinking again and thus gave his wife cause to sue for divorce.

He did not mention the extenuating circumstance of his emotional and legal tribulations until the deteriorating quality of his service was complained of.

Hereward, who was more often at home and lived at closer quarters to Brownie than Jacques, was the first to realise something was amiss. Brownie's breath began to smell of beer or alcohol – occasionally the whole upper floor of the maisonette smelt like a brewery. The white jackets he wore got grubbier, he took less trouble with his clothes, and another odour of stale sweat and dirty socks emanated from his bedroom, the door of which he now kept locked. He was apt to become unnaturally talkative and sentimental : 'Lord Tatters Tatham was the best of the bunch at the Piccadilly Club. I'd have gone through hell and fire-water for Lord Tatters!' He had a TV set in the kitchen : he would drop off to sleep in front of it and disturb Hereward in the adjoining room with his thunderous snores. After dinner parties downstairs, the process of washing up, and crashing and banging of cutlery and crockery, would continue into the small hours.

His cooking was no longer what it had been. At those dinner parties, the meat was cold and the ice-cream was hot, there were extended intervals between courses, and he took it on himself to converse in a loud voice with the guests as he served them: 'Breast or thigh, Madame? You'll find a dear tender piece of breast by your right hand, Madame. And you must have lashings of my speciality *sauce de tomates* with *cognac* . . . It's thigh for you, isn't it, my lord? You gobble up your thigh, my lord, and I'll slip you a second helping . . .'

At length Jacques issued a mild rebuke in general terms. He too had his suspicions, he had been surprised by the amount of drink consumed on the premises, but did not like to broach such an awkward subject. Brownie confessed his sins. That is to say he described his marital catastrophe and apologised for having let it interfere with his work. He thanked Jacques for drawing attention to his absent-mindedness and promised faithfully that he would never have reason to do so in the future.

He was more or less believed, and steps were immediately taken to assist him through the temporary crisis.

*

Jacques acted on Hereward's theory that Brownie might be overworked. He engaged a daily lady to clean the rooms on his floor of the maisonette. She was Polish, called Mrs Kowscko, sixty-ish, squat and rotund. Brownie flirted with her, said she was more like a calf than a cow, relieved her of any job she considered doing, and soon demoralised her.

Mrs Kowscko began to arrive at eleven o'clock instead of nine, carrying several empty shopping bags and just in time for coffee and cakes in the kitchen. She dawdled over her coffee until twelve, laughing at and with Brownie. Then they adjourned to Jacques' flat, where they played games with their feather dusters. At one she returned to the kitchen for a square meal and at two she departed with her shopping bags bulging.

The household bills soared. Brownie did not hesitate to point the finger at Mrs Kowscko, who in her turn accused him of every crime under the sun. The next daily lady employed by Jacques was Mrs Whitworth, a severe middle-aged Scot.

Brownie's flirting took a different form. He told Mrs Whitworth that his mother had been a Macgregor, pronouncing the name with a marked Scottish accent, and he was ex-Black Watch. He softened her up by appealing to her nationalistic sentiments – Windle Road rang with his 'Och ayes!' and 'Och noes!' And he so brainwashed her, probably by exaggerating the demands made upon him – 'I'm butler, valet, cook, house-maid, telephone operator and errand-boy rolled into one: I'm on duty sixteen hours a day!' – that she could not speak civilly to Jacques or Hereward, whom she must have regarded as ruthless slave-drivers.

Luckily she had to leave for some reason. Brownie's un-expected attitude was – good riddance. For Mrs Whitworth was a secret dipsomaniac, he declared. His answer to the question of Monsieur Beausson's disappearing drink was that it had been poured down her throat.

Jacques' experiments in easing his manservant's lot by physical means were obvious failures. Brownie never could work with other people: he was too much of a perfectionist, in a sense too pernicketty, and he spoilt them, and was demoralised by as well as demoralising them. And he was unable to resist an opportunity to whitewash his own character by blackening theirs. It was almost inconceivable the dour brisk Mrs Whitworth was a dipsomaniac, or that Mrs Kowscko pinched a ton of food without his connivance. But his calumnies were nonetheless advantageous from his point of view. For they divided, if not removed, Jacques' suspicions in respect of the bottles on the drink-tray. And his boss ran no more risks with meddlesome daily ladies, who might or might not be bad influences.

No – clearly – assistance would have to be moral, psychological, verbal – and specific and straightforward, too.

Brownie's crisis was not so temporary as had been hoped. A year of it had already passed, his divorce was dragging on, and he was behaving more oddly than ever. Gone were the dinner party days when he was ready half an hour before the guests arrived – everything under control in the kitchen, the table laid with gleaming silver and glass, the wine decanted, and himself freshly shaved in a pristine jacket, his face pink and shiny, exuding health and happiness, and none of his five hundred thousand brain-cells filled with beeswax. Instead, frenetic and flustered, interrupting his last minute arrangements to plunge downstairs in response to the doorbell, breathless, his eyes popping and rolling, he under-cooked and over-cooked his party pieces and handed them round on wobbly platters, startling strangers with his muttered expletives – 'Mamma mia! Jesus!' etcetera; and was liable to fall asleep with his head on the kitchen table after serving the coffee weak and lukewarm.

Jacques protested.

Excessive drinkers put their real friends in an intolerable position. While drunkards wreak havoc in the lives of their nearest and dearest, the borderline cases create dilemmas. How addicted are they? Should somebody butt in before it is too late? Will disagreeable advice be understood, accepted, forgiven – or any use? Does one have the nerve to advise? Does one have the right? Yet rectitude cannot be equated with standing by and even negatively co-operating as a valuable person one is fond of goes to the dogs.

Jacques had been loath to stray into such an ethical mine-field. He worked extremely hard in order to earn money partly to pay a manservant who would save him trouble – not make it. He had no energy to spare to fight on the home-front for Brownie's sobriety, and was disinclined to break the rule of his reserve.

But nature stepped in. Nature alone rescues us from the horns of horrid dilemmas. A combination of disappointment and irritation inspired him to speak out.

On a typical morning after the night before, he summoned Brownie and charged him with drunkenness.

'Oh no, sir – not that – I'm sorry you should think that, sir – it's not true, I promise – I've signed the pledge, sir – I swear it on the grave of my dear mother!'

Brownie was deeply shocked by the imputation. He rebutted it with tears in his eyes. Not a single drop of strong liquor had crossed his lips since he had been in Monsieur Beausson's employ. Moreover, if he had been drinking, he would never have touched the drink that belonged to Monsieur Beausson. He was not a thief! But he laughed at the whole idea – and invoked the members of his family in the Salvation Army, who had persuaded him to sign that teetotal pledge long ago. Not only his mother, but God Almighty Himself, were his witnesses!

Jacques was taken aback.

Brownie hurried on: 'I've been receiving nasty letters from my wife, sir. I know I promised not to let her get me down. But she's vicious, sir. You wouldn't believe the wicked lies she writes about me – they choke me, they do, and I can't settle to my duties as I should. Your good self and Mr Watkins have shown me nothing but kindness. May I ask you to be kind and patient for a little longer – just until my divorce is through and I'm less upset?'

Jacques began to apologise.

'Please, sir – it's all right, sir – I quite appreciate how you came to be mistaken,' Brownie said with magnanimity. 'And I'll try hard to keep my spirits up and give satisfaction. Will there be anything else, sir?'

Jacques managed not to capitulate completely. He had been bitten once before and was twice shy.

He wanted all his drink locked in the cupboard under the stairs.

'I'll do it now, sir. I was going to suggest it myself.'

Brownie carried the bottles in question into the cupboard, stacked them regimentally on the wine-racks, locked the door with an ostentatious flourish and presented the key to his boss.

Later the same day he relapsed into his woolly woozy state.

*

Brownie won his divorce and lost his excuse. But his daughter married, he said he had to fork out more money than he could afford for the wedding, and his debts became the scapegoat for his erratic conduct. When his debts were paid with the help of Jacques, he produced a new alibi in the person of a favourite brother who was dying by slow degrees: 'Mick's in pain, sir – I can't concentrate for thinking of his pain.' In between times, he claimed he was seriously ill with

59

'flu, toothache, conjunctivitis, lumbago and housemaid's knee. And he still had a trump card up his sleeve.

Hereward took over from where Jacques had left off.

He had recently published his first novel, which was successful, and was invited to attend a public reading from it. Brownie agreed to iron his suit for the occasion, at which he needed to look smart. He dressed in a hurry on the night, and arrived and mingled with the readers and the audience. He noticed a bad smell, and that the people who were introduced to him recoiled with expressions of embarrassment and disgust on their faces. He realised his suit was responsible for the stink – and tackled Brownie with the spontaneity of anger on the following day.

'What did you do to my best suit? No – don't tell me a lot of fibs! I'll tell you: you used a filthy washing-up towel as a damp cloth when you ironed it – you impregnated it with grease and detergent – you ruined it – and you made a proper fool of me at my function – I might as well have stepped straight out of a sewer. I suppose you'd been drinking again?'

As usual Brownie denied everything.

He had not been drinking; the towel he had used as a damp cloth was cleaner than any whistle; the suit had been as smelly as hell before he touched it – he had had to hold his nose while doing the job; but had simply obeyed Mr Watkins' orders, weighed down with work for Monsieur Beausson though he was – and so on.

Another incident provoked Hereward to speak his mind. If he was spending the weekend alone at Windle Road, Brownie would leave him snacks of cold food in the kitchen. The snacks were laid out appetisingly under sheets of greaseproof paper and the kitchen always appeared to be spotless.

But one weekend Hereward, instead of removing the paper and consuming the food according to custom, decided to cook himself some hot sphaghetti. He reached for the middle-sized saucepan of the set on a saucepan-stand and lifted the lid: it contained the mildewed remains of stewed cabbage. None of the saucepans on the stand, which were burnished on the outside, had been emptied or cleaned. He opened the drawer reserved for kitchen implements – they had been thrown in dirty. He explored further and found stacks of unwashed plates, teapots full of stale tea, blackened frying-pans with fat in them, broken dishes galore, and squalid souvenirs of dinner parties, greenish *pommes fantastiques* in a lipsticked wine glass, a half-eaten *Croque Monsieur* swimming in a bowl of cherries with kirsch.

He duly vented his wrath on Brownie.

'Your kitchen's a disgrace. Look at this, look at that! Do you want to poison us? It's revolting – and I know why, even if you pretend you don't! You're going all to pieces because of drink!'

Brownie professed amazement at the sights he was made to see – 'I'd no idea it was that bad, sir.' However, he reminded Hereward that the previous week had been particularly busy and that he had stayed at his post, cooking dinners, on duty for sixteen hours a day, although fearful his brother would expire before he was at liberty to dash to the hospital. What with being worked so hard, and Mick at death's door, and his rotten tooth and his gammy knee, he had not felt up to tidying the kitchen properly. Of course he would give it a thorough blitz at once. It would be ready for inspection in a couple of hours. As for drink, he repeated that he did not partake.

Hereward was unconvinced. On the other hand he had to

admit that his evidence was circumstantial, not to say flimsy. He had never caught Brownie in the act of partaking. He was impressed in spite of himself by the consistency of Brownie's denials.

In a word, he was gullible. In retrospect he was staggered by his gullibility. He had been slow in the uptake, as he was to see Brownie's jokes.

'The trouble is,' he used to say, 'Brownie's cleverer than me. He's always been a jump ahead, and for all I know he is still.'

And Hereward meant it, although most of his friends scoffed at such false modesty.

Certainly his aristocratic compassion for a dependent at the opposite end of the social scale, and hereditary feudal concern for a servant on whom he depended, were played upon by that essential craft of the lower classes which Brownie carried to the point of virtuosity. He was induced to feel guilty by hints of Brownie having to work too hard, of the consequent deterioration of Brownie's health, of Brownie having been divorced because of his devotion to duty, and his being denied access to the deathbed of his brother. Guilt tied Hereward's hands as intended, inhibiting his scepticism – and Jacques': for instance, since they as bosses could be the bone of contention between Brownie and his wife, neither of them liked to demand to see her vicious letters which he said were his undoing. Over the episodes of the stinking suit and the discovery of disaster areas in the kitchen, Hereward was at even more of a disadvantage, considering he had asked Brownie to iron his suit – a favour, and extra work, not specifically paid for – and he happened to be snooping in the kitchen because of Brownie's snacks, which came into the same gratuitous category. He had enjoyed those snacks, the preparation of which was part of Brownie's particularly busy week that might have prevented him from bidding his beloved brother farewell – and was therefore obliged to restrain an indignation deriving from his enjoyment, ungrateful and stony-hearted.

Again, notwithstanding his blue blood and anachronistic attitudes, Hereward was sufficiently imbued or infected with the spirit of the age not to want to seem to be grinding the face of the poor.

Yet again, as a normally truthful person, he could not conceive of Brownie's total disregard for the truth.

The resultant paradox was that he was exploited by Brownie, at least in a moral sense, rather than the other way round.

The only weak spot in Brownie's subtly aggressive defences, behind which he lived his private life and kept his secrets, was his charm. His chief strength, his amusing engaging infinitely plausible personality, was also his weakness: it was like a parable.

For Hereward had grown fond of him. He would miss a great deal more than menial services if Jacques decided to get rid of Brownie. He could not bear to stand by and take a detached spectator's view of the possession of his friend and in many respects his benefactor by evil forces.

He joined in the battle for Brownie's soul – or at any rate for his physical salvation and his job.

*

One morning he was too worked up over the situation at Windle Road to be able to write. He interrupted his rigid routine and went for a walk. And he ran into Brownie, who emerged from a pub in a back alley.

'What were you doing there?'

'Trying to buy half a bottle of cheap red wine for cooking, sir.'

'Why didn't you buy it from the grocer?'

'I forgot, sir.'

'Sorry – I don't believe that. I believe you were drinking.'

'No, sir – never.'

'Shall I check with the landlord?'

'I might have had a Guinness, sir. My doctor advised me to.'

'What about your pledge? What about all your swearing to me and Monsieur Beausson that you don't drink?'

'I only do it sometimes – under doctor's orders.'

'How often is sometimes? Every day?'

'If possible, sir, so as to keep fit.'

'You drink Guinness on most days – is that your story now?'

'Yes, sir – just a glass, sir.'

'You fool, Brownie! You're not yourself, you're making yourself sick, because you guzzle Guinness – don't you understand? Your doctor ought to be struck off the register if he really gave you that advice. Well, at last we know roughly where we are. I've caught you at it, because you thought I was writing and you were safe – and you'll have to stop. Obviously drink's been the problem all along. I'll help you. Instead of lying and lying, you should have let me help you before. As it is you're halfway down the drain.'

'Yes, sir.'

'Do you agree?'

'I'm sure I can pull back, sir.'

'Are you willing to have a shot?'

'Oh yes, sir! I agree it's not been good for me, in spite of the advertisements.'

'Seriously, Brownie?'

'Yes, sir.'

'In that case I won't say anything to Monsieur Beausson. We'll see what we can do together.'

'Thank you, sir.'

Brownie's thanks, and misleading passivity and malleability, his yielding to pressure in accordance with the theory of ju-jitsu, and then his reformations which were short-lived, lured Hereward deeper into the fray. He was an expert flatterer – and nothing flatters a person more than the idea that he or she can save the soul of another.

Hereward was pleased to think he had established a little bridgehead of truth : namely that Brownie drank Guinness in pubs and was willing to co-operate with a team-effort to curtail his alcoholic activity.

And perhaps Brownie was in earnest when – or whenever – he volunteered co-operation. Addicts are supposed to long to be free of their addiction. But he had been issued with the sort of challenge he could not resist. The more Hereward supervised and investigated his movements, where he was, what he was up to, whether or not he had had time to sink a Guinness, the more elusive and evasive he became. He began to drink not only because he needed to – also to put one over on his authoritarian mentor.

Hereward raged unrestrainedly now, as at a partner who had let him down. He threatened to divulge the secret they shared to Jacques, painted grim pictures of Brownie's future if he got the sack, tried conciliatory tactics, appealed to better feelings, gave innumerable pep talks and extracted as many solemn promises.

He was frustrated, exasperated, and in his exasperation

inclined to go too far – thus making the very mistake he sought to correct, if verbally as opposed to alcoholically.

Again he caught Brownie emerging from a pub, inebriated beyond the shadow of a doubt.

'How could you?' he demanded.

'Oh, sir – I couldn't help it, sir – I heard today that my brother had to have his leg off.'

'You've always got some feeble excuse,' Hereward retorted.

He apologised afterwards. He had to apologise almost as often as Brownie did. His nerves were stretched near to breaking-point as the battle wore on.

In several of their skirmishes his defeats were mysterious. Since so many promises had been broken, he broke his and confided in Jacques. Between them they concocted a generally beneficial plot. In the course of a weekend, in Brownie's absence, Hereward thoroughly and in vain searched the kitchen for drink. On the Monday morning Jacques asked for and received every possible assurance that Brownie had no drink hidden in his locked bedroom. Jacques then accompanied Brownie to the shops to buy things for his dinner party in the evening. For the rest of the day, during which Brownie was forbidden to leave the premises, Hereward kept a sharp eye on him. Jacques, home from work, retrieved the bottles from the cupboard under the stairs and decanted the wine, and later he himself charged the glasses of his guests.

Brownie passed out nonetheless between the meat and the pudding.

Where, when and how had he obtained the means?

It might have been in connection with that episode, as inexplicable as it was inexcusable, that he played his trump card – or suggested he had such a trump literally up his sleeve. Under interrogation he referred to his tumours. He rolled the sleeve of his shirt to the elbow and displayed the lumps in his forearm.

He would recall that his mother had died in screaming agony of a tumour behind her eye and say he had been having headaches which frightened him out of his wits. He implied that his behaviour could in no way be accounted for, except by a tumour forming in his brain – and if so he was the innocent victim of a terrible error on the part of his bosses, who should pity instead of persecuting him.

More than likely he was crying wolf as before, although louder. Yet the mysteriousness of his addiction or disease or whatever it was tended to reinforce his latest threat – or defensive response to threats. He would pop round to the tobacconist's for a packet of Woodbines and return drunk in a matter of five minutes. He would trip lightly down the stairs to lay the table for a party and soon hardly be able to stumble up. And his health was unquestionably going to pot, Hereward's remedial efforts notwithstanding. He was at once thin and puffy round the jowls, and heavy-eyed, with none of his former zeal and zip. His clothes were slovenly and his kitchen past praying for.

Early one morning there was a commotion in the kitchen, shouts, curses, sounds of furniture being manhandled and breaking glass.

'What's happening, Brownie?'

'I've got a rat in here.'

'You've got a what?'

'A blasted rat, sir! It's as big as a dachshund!'

'What are you doing to it?'

'I'm shying milk bottles at it.'

Esoteric swear-words were heard, followed by a bang and the tinkle of more breaking glass.

Hereward and Jacques hurried to join Brownie, who was sweating profusely and trembling.

'Where is this rat?'

'It just went behind the fridge.'

'Right – I'll pull the fridge away from the wall and you two get ready to wallop it with brooms – okay?'

But the rat had vanished.

'I saw it, sir – large as life – it had a nasty sneering sort of expression – honestly, sir!'

'Where did it come from?'

'It stepped in through the window – it marched along the parapet outside and jumped in – it looked me straight in the eye – I'm not exaggerating, sir!'

'Well, it seems to have made itself scarce. I wouldn't worry any more, Brownie. You'd better clear up all the mess.'

The rat could have been real or a sad hallucination due to a brain tumour. But Brownie's bosses veered towards the opinion that it was a figment of his befuddled imagination – in other words he had had an attack of *delirium tremens*.

*

The climax occurred in the ninth year of the triangular arrangement at Windle Road.

Jacques gave a dinner party for Colonel de Chiffre, who was staying in his spare room. Hereward, having spent the evening out with friends, returned at ten o'clock and was climbing the maisonette stairs to the top floor. Brownie lurched from the kitchen bearing the main course on a platter – a loveable duck dissected, *pommes fantastiques* and vegetables. He was intoxicated. On the landing he subsided quite slowly onto one knee, while the platter tipped and pieces of duck slid off it and gravy dripped on the carpet and the miniature roast potato balls bounced down the staircase.

And gazing at Hereward horror-struck he mumbled: 'Oh sir – what will Monsieur le Colonel say?'

In the morning there was the worst row ever. But Brownie was about to go on his annual holiday. He managed to persuade everyone that after a fortnight's rest he would be a different person.

He departed, leaving his kitchen looking like a bomb-site and his bedroom locked. Hereward worked for two days at cleaning the kitchen, and then on an angry impulse swung himself through the window onto the parapet where the rat had marched, and edged along and peered into Brownie's room. Fifty or a hundred empty bottles of wine and spirits lay all over the floor. The bed was unmade – the sheets were greenish-brown. Putrid socks, shirts, trousers and shoes were scattered amongst the bottles. The washbasin was encrusted with grime.

Brownie's holiday did him no good. He had only the vaguest recollection of the places he had visited. Somewhere he had gone in for horseback riding: he said his legs were stiff and chafed and walked with them bowed like a cowboy.

But Jacques and Hereward were not in the mood for jokes. Jacques reminded Brownie of the fiasco of that last party, and complained of the shambles of his bedroom and his tipsy homecoming. He ran through the history of their association and what he had put up with. He declared that now Brownie must agree to see his – Jacques' – doctor and submit to treatment, or else they would have to part.

Brownie demurred once more. He dreaded the medical profession, which, he asserted, went berserk with excitement on catching a glimpse of the rarity of his tumours. He related that in the past he had consulted a doctor about a stye in his eye, was ordered to undress completely and ushered stark naked on to the stage in a theatre crammed with students. At Windle Road he had always recoiled from professional investigation of the various maladies he said he suffered from.

But he was hoisted on the petard of his recent inflation of those maladies. He could not warn his employer he was dangerously ill and refuse a request to prove it. He had to choose between accepting a condition he himself had caused to be imposed on his continued service, and dismissal from his job for drunkenness.

He saw Jacques' doctor, who sent him to hospital for tests. Apparently his liver, kidneys, blood, digestion and nerves were in a shocking state. Almost the only thing that was not wrong with him was his brain. He was advised, and received permission and encouragement from Jacques and Hereward, to do the necessary cure.

It seemed to be successful. Two months later, back at work, he did seem to have become a different person – pink-cheeked, clear-eyed, slim, no longer puffy, calm, clean, stronger and more active. He was full of the doctors, nurses and other patients in the hospital, who had thought the world of him.

He kept it up for about a fortnight.

As soon as he relapsed, Jacques announced that he had had enough.

Then Jacques was recalled to work in the head-office of his bank in France.

And at the same time the landlords of Windle Road realised they were charging too little for the maisonette and doubled the rent.

Brownie would be unemployed. Hereward was losing his

tenant, and had neither the financial resources nor the temerity to assume sole responsibility for a new expensive lease of his home. Jacques packed his belongings.

After ten years together they all prepared to go their separate ways.

4

Jacques said goodbye, and arranged for his pieces of furniture to be removed from his flat, including the bookcase that had stood in the entrance hall.

The removal of the bookcase uncovered a two-foot-square hinged grille into the cupboard under the stairs in which Jacques had carefully locked his wine and spirits.

'Well, fancy that, Brownie!' Hereward commented. 'One mystery's solved at any rate. Now I know how and where you got hold of your drink without leaving the house. You just shifted the bookcase and reached in for it. And I used to think you were cleaning when I heard you banging about down here. You're too crafty by half – helping Monsieur Beausson to put his bottles out of harm's way and making such a palaver with the key – and having your own secret door into the cupboard all the time!'

Brownie pretended to be surprised by the revelation of the grille.

'But didn't you ever move the bookcase in order to dust behind it?' Hereward persisted. 'Either you were aware of the existence of a second door, and therefore in a position to open it and get at the booze, or you weren't doing the dusting part of your job properly.'

'I must have slipped up on the dusting, sir,' Brownie decided with a shifty giggle.

There had been no recurrence of his one relapse too many following his cure. He was still reeling from the implementation of the repetitive threat in which he had ceased to believe – irreversible now that Jacques was in France. He could not count on a blameless reference from his ex-boss. His future in his mid-forties was to say the least uncertain. He was probably trying hard not to compromise it further.

Hereward was paying his wages in the meanwhile, but explained that he could only afford to do so on a temporary basis.

He was a stricter employer than Jacques: he had more opportunities to be strict since he worked at home; maybe he was more dogged, more determined to win the battle for Brownie's well-being, or more competitive, more reluctant to admit he was beaten; and naturally he wanted to receive full value for the greater proportion of his income – and indeed capital – he was investing in Brownie's services.

The combination of his own abstemiousness and his shortage of cash to spend on alcoholic beverages for guests meant that Brownie was not exposed to temptation as he had been He did not give parties. He did not have people to stay. He did not like to eat food flavoured with strange herbs unobtainable except in Soho. He attempted to lead a quiet regular life. Moreover he was English and had been in the army, he had a native understanding and some experience of the type of man he was dealing with, just as he was understood for the same reasons. He was also accessible and easy to talk to.

All this was good for Brownie, who began to demonstrate his trust in Hereward – whether or not his motives were as ambiguous as usual.

He described his time in hospital in more detail.

'They had genuine alcoholics there. They shut the worst ones in padded cells. We used to hear them howling and doing their best to bash their brains out.'

'That can't have been very nice.'

'We howled right back at them. We told them to put a sock in it. They were stupid. They smuggled in drink if they could. They bribed the nurses and porters to bring them drink. They couldn't think of nothing else. A terrible lot of drinking went on in the place.'

'Did you partake?'

'No, sir.'

Sometimes he spoke sympathetically of his fellow-patients.

'We got every sort in hospital, company directors, top executives – you'd be amazed. We had a vicar with letters after his name. He was the most pleasant gentleman you could meet in a day's march. His wife and his children had left him, and he'd lost his money and his house and his job – he was sacked for being paralytic in the pulpit. He said he drank anything – communion wine, meths, cider laced with the white spirit painters wash their brushes in, women's perfume. He'd drunk his whole life away.'

'I hope he taught you a lesson, Brownie.'

'Yes, sir. But I couldn't help feeling sorry for him. He was teetotal until he was forty. Then an old lady in his parish gave him a recipe for making wine from cowslips. He tried it, he got interested in making wine, and five years later he found himself in a padded cell.'

As a rule Brownie's reminiscences were less morbid.

'I did a spot of PT in the mornings, fed like a fighting cock, lazed around in the afternoons with the telly blasting, and in the evenings I played snooker with my Dr Martin. He was a beautiful doctor, sir. He thought I was the pig's whiskers.'

74

'You really enjoyed your cure, didn't you?'

'I did, sir – really.'

The latter statement was tinged with doubt.

'Was your treatment nasty?'

'No, not too bad, except for the electric shocks.'

'Did they give you electric shocks?'

'Oh yes, sir – I must have had half a dozen.'

'But what on earth for?'

'For my condition. I wasn't on the alcoholic side, sir. It was a hospital for nervous diseases with the alcoholics on one side and the rest of us in a separate building on the other. Dr Martin diagnosed my condition the minute he set eyes on me. He said I was nowhere near an alcoholic.'

'What did he say you were?'

'Schizophrenic, sir.'

'But, Brownie, you're no more schizophrenic than I am! That's ridiculous!'

'That's what he said, sir.'

'Did he talk to you? Did he go into your case thoroughly? I mean – did you talk to him?'

'Oh yes, sir, we had some long talks.'

'Well, you obviously tied him in knots if he was persuaded that your problem was schizophrenia. What else did he do to you apart from the electric shocks?'

'I had insulin, sir. I was in a coma for a couple of weeks. They pumped insulin into me and just woke me up to eat. I had to eat two meals at a time to counteract the insulin – two breakfasts of grapefruit, porridge, egg, bacon, sausage, a rack of six rounds of toast with lashings of butter and marmalade, washed down by a pint of white coffee – and the same again with lunch and tea and dinner.'

'How could you swallow so much food?'

'It was the dope, sir. I could have swallowed a horse. My appetite was awful.'

'Brownie – I still can't quite believe in the electric shocks. What were they like?'

'I was taken along to a kind of operating theatre. They fixed wires to my head and plugged me in. Afterwards I couldn't walk straight. I felt as if I'd had a few jars.'

'When did you begin to mend?'

'When they cut me off the insulin, sir. A nurse took me for walks in the hospital grounds with a packet of biscuits in her pocket. She handed me a biscuit if I got drowsy. Without the biscuit I would have slipped back into a coma. Dr Martin was very pleased with my progress.'

'I bet he was, considering he was treating you for a disease you didn't have.'

*

Hereward reverted to the topic.

'Listen – I'm bewildered by your account of what happened to you in hospital. You arrived there with alcohol coming out of your ears – and say you had to undergo a completely unnecessary cure for schizophrenia. My guess is that you talked yourself into the wrong stream on purpose. Didn't you even mention your drinking to Dr Martin? Did he have nothing to say about that?'

'He said it was a symptom of the schizophrenia, sir.'

'But schizophrenia means a split personality. Schizophrenics who require electric shocks are more or less up the pole. You must have played a pretty funny game with your Dr Martin. Did you put any other bright ideas into his head?'

'No, sir.'

'He passed you fit when you'd recovered from his treatment?'

'Yes, sir. I was over my malnutrition by then.'

'Malnutrition? What next, Brownie? I should think you had got over it with your double breakfasts and so on! But for heaven's sake – this house was knee-deep in stuff to eat when Monsieur Beausson threw parties. You can't convince me you were starved here.'

'I didn't bother to feed myself if I was on the sherbet, sir.'

'When you were on the sherbet – not if you were on it.'

'Yes, sir.'

'Well – now you're sober, and not under-nourished, and have been treated for schizophrenia, can you tell me why you let drink get the upper hand of you and ruin your prospects?'

'I mixed in bad company.'

'In pubs, you mean?'

'Not only in pubs. Those chefs in the hotel where I was sent for cooking lessons, they drank like a shoal of fishes. And you remember Madame Drey? She drank enough to sink a battleship – although she was so thin you could have sliced bacon with her. She killed a bottle of whisky stone dead during each of our sessions in the kitchen. And then the cleaning lady Mrs Whitworth – she was a wild beast for drink.'

'Are you suggesting nothing was your fault?'

'No, sir – but they got me going. Afterwards, when I was worried or needed cheering up, I was inclined to have one.'

'Or two or three.'

'Yes, sir.'

'What puzzles me is that you seem to be far more cheerful without drink than you ever were with it.'

'I know. I've been the biggest fool. But I've registered the message at last. And as they say, sir – better late than never.'

'Well – yes – I agree – and I don't want to bully you or rake

77

over the past. But the most important question for both of us is whether the hospital produced any permanent late solutions, and if you're likely to feel in need of cheering up in the future.'

'I won't, sir – that I can promise you. I've seen the light, I swear.'

'Please don't swear, Brownie, whatever else you do. If you begin to swear, I'll be sure you're lying.'

Ambiguity must be contagious. Hereward had caught a dose of it. For while he sternly lectured and pedantically corrected and preached the virtues of sobriety in such conversations, he was half-hoping Brownie would get drunk again. In that case he could point to the failure of every experiment, and, following Jacques' example as an employer, call it a day. With justification he could lay down the moral and financial burden of Brownie – and concentrate on the more vital business of supporting himself.

His hope was disappointed. Butter would not have melted in Brownie's mouth in this interim period. He was subdued and acquiescent, alert, willing, and never caused embarrassment by enquiring into his boss's plans in the longer term. He conveyed the impression that he relied absolutely on Hereward, who was thus the more embroiled in his destiny.

Occasionally the past was raked over, in spite of Hereward's stated wish – or rather the past had its effect on the present. Why had it taken Brownie two hours to buy an evening paper – had he been up to his old tricks – how was he ever to be trusted – and how could he expect anyone to pay wages for the pleasure of being kept on tenterhooks? Brownie would establish his innocence without reproaching Hereward for injuring it. He was sad not be be given the benefit of the doubt he now deserved – he might shed a few crocodile tears – but quick to accept an apology and forgive and forget. His policy resembled the military strategy of coaxing an invader so deep into your territory that he cannot retreat.

Hereward had an uneasy feeling he was being subjected to Brownie's patent process, which converted masters into servants. To sack him as it were in cold blood was becoming increasingly difficult. To advance the base argument of money – or the lack of it – as the reason to terminate their close sort of friendship went against the grain. The passage of each impeccable week reinforced the extravagant notion of their having to sink or swim together.

Moreover Hereward was obliged to admit that Brownie was his chief material asset, if not his only one. He had been cossetted for ten years, and enabled to write his books without too many interruptions, by Brownie. Supposing he provided a roof over their heads, it was just conceivable that he could market the talents and some of the time of his man-servant, while they continued to enjoy the apparently mutual benefits of co-habitation.

There were two large stumbling-blocks in the way of the scheme.

The prices and rents of suitable accommodation were prohibitive.

And no outsider was going to pay Brownie a penny for being drunk and disorderly.

Hereward's predicament was frightening. A roof over his own head, let alone Brownie's, seemed to be beyond his means. In the unlikely event of his finding a dirt-cheap flat with the right number of rooms, he could not guarantee that Brownie would not turn into his chief liability. As it was, day by day, he was squandering his resources on a maisonette in the West End that was far too big for him, and on a butler-cum-valet-cum-cook who was equally above his financial station. He saw himself on the bread-line round the next corner, dragging Brownie after him like a ball and chain.

Then the same kind sister who had encouraged him to lease Windle Road came to the rescue. She was keen for him to buy a house for sale in a cul-de-sac in Hampstead. It was again a bargain, dilapidated yet potentially desirable, quiet and yet close to shops and bus-routes, and had a basement he could let. She offered to contribute to the purchase price.

He was touched by her generosity, grateful and hesitant. The house was of a size which frightened him almost as much as the prospect of homelessness. He would not be able to live there, and carry on writing, without practical daily help: which raised the question of Brownie in a more vexatious pressing form.

The fortunes of the Watkins family were mobilised in support of the project. Hereward's mother promised to chip in with money, and another sister with furniture. But he still hesitated.

He sought guidance everywhere. Should he commit himself to the swings and roundabouts of a haven in Hampstead plus Brownie? Or should he get rid of Brownie, repudiate extraneous responsibilities, travel light, and look for a lonely garret in the suburbs?

He discussed his quandary with an acquaintance, Dr White, a qualified psychiatrist, who told him categorically to steer clear of lame ducks at all costs.

The consensus of hard-headed opinion was that sooner or later Brownie was bound to be reclaimed by his alcoholic habits.

Eventually Hereward reached his independent decision.

He showed Brownie the house and asked if he would like to work there. He explained his finances fully – what revenue he could depend on, what rent from a basement tenant he hoped for, what annual salary he might rustle up. He proposed that if Brownie settled for Hampstead he should take time off as required to do dinners and odd jobs for other people in order to supplement his income. He said he refused to believe that history always repeats itself – he was therefore ready to gamble on Brownie sticking to the straight and narrow. The single string attached to the job was total abstinence.

Brownie was relieved and excited. He brushed aside Hereward's reminder that he could probably obtain more remunerative employment elsewhere. No other boss would be so good and kind, he declared.

On the strength of his reaction the deal was clinched with estate agents and lawyers.

That evening Brownie celebrated.

*

The following morning Hereward broke his word.

At least he suspended the condition of abstinence he had insisted on, and Brownie had accepted, the previous day. He was afraid his decision had been wrong, that Dr White and company had already been proved right, and he was now compounding his wilful foolish behaviour with his weakness. But his heart was not hard enough to be impervious to exceptionally contrite and credible appeals for one more chance. And he was reluctant to cancel all his elaborate plans twenty-four hours after he had put them into operation.

For better or worse Brownie looked at the matter from a different point of view. As he seemed to see it, Hereward was honouring his word under stress and re-affirming his trust and faith in the penitent sinner he was raising to the status of an indispensable colleague. Brownie was not only grateful and gratified, he was also confronted by the challenge of his new master's attitude: he too could act like a proper gentleman.

He said: 'I'll pay you back, sir – you'll never regret it!' – which hackneyed assurances were remarkable in that they were nearly true.

The above sequence of events – Hereward's creation of a future for Brownie notwithstanding his awareness of the risks he ran: Brownie's instant destructiveness which Hereward chose not to penalise although entitled to – was a watershed in their story.

From then on water figured in it more than ever before. Brownie actually began to drink water when he was thirsty, or tea or coffee to cheer himself up. He grew more confidential the more he was certain he could have confidence in someone who had confidence in him. He substantiated the claim that Hereward had saved his life.

'I was drinking more than I let on, sir. I was horrible. I couldn't get out of bed in the morning without a snifter.'

'What of?'

'Whisky or vodka.'

'What do you call a snifter?'

'Well, a snifter's a snort, and a snort's a miniature.'

'I'm sorry – I don't understand – what's a miniature?'

'A miniature bottle, sir.'

'Don't those miniature bottles come in various sizes?'

'Yes, sir. I drank the sort that's half the size of a whole bottle.'

'You drank half a bottle of whisky or vodka before breakfast?'

'It was my breakfast, sir. I shouldn't think I ate a decent meal in three years. I couldn't fancy food. I didn't seem to need it – alcohol's nourishing, they say. But not eating played

Old Harry with my insides and my nerves and the rest of me. Dr Martin said I was rotten right through at my first examination. He would have given me six months if I hadn't been treated in hospital. And if you'd given me the push the other day, sir, I definitely would have started again and drunk myself under ground.'

'What happened to you after drinking half a bottle of spirits for breakfast?'

'I kept topped up.'

'How?'

'In pubs, when I was meant to be shopping. I bought drink in off-licences, too.'

'And brought it home?'

'Yes, sir.'

'I knew you did. I knew you had it somewhere – and used to search for it at weekends and at other times when you weren't around. I found lots of empties, for instance in your bedroom during your last holiday, but never what I was looking for.'

'I hid it, sir. You remember the milk bottles I washed and lined alongside my sink? You probably thought there was water in them. In fact it was vodka or gin.'

He referred to that holiday which led to his final collapse and hospitalisation: 'It was crazy. One day I was supping cider in Somerset and the next I was riding horseback in the Isle of Wight. I couldn't have told you where I was or how I got there. I slept on beaches or in public parks. And every night I believed I'd wake up dead in the morning.'

He reminisced about his former involvement with the charity called The Blind Scribe.

'We collected money for it in a Working Men's Club I belonged to down Plumstead way. We organised weekly raffles, and on a Saturday every year we hired a coach and took a load of blind guests to a beauty spot, Canterbury Cathedral, or the tulip fields in Lincolnshire.'

'But the blind people couldn't see the tulips.'

'None of us could, sir. We were all intoxicated by the time we reached our destination. The coach pulled in at roadside pubs. After half a dozen pubs our guests were paralysed as well. We had an awful job, hauling them back to their seats.'

'Talk of the blind leading the blind!'

Brownie giggled ruefully and added: 'They loved the outing, sir. They laughed and sang, although once we got an awkward so-and-so who tried to batter somebody's head in with his white stick. It was just a bit of fun.'

'Tell me – what was your tipple in these innumerable pubs you patronised?'

'Ales and stout, sir – Guinness – and chasers. Often the chasers came in ahead of the ales and stout.'

'Is a chaser neat spirits?'

'Yes, sir.'

'What did you use for money?'

'I was in terrible debt. I owed money everywhere. When I was too skint for chasers I concentrated on beer. Now I can't stand a man on the beer near me – the stench makes me want to vomit. I wonder you didn't complain, sir.'

'I did, Brownie.'

'Sorry, sir.'

In the course of the move from Windle Road he showed Hereward an ornamental tankard he was about to pack.

He said it was a prize.

'What for?'

'Drinking.'

'How much did you drink to win it?'

'Twenty-one pints.'

'You're joking!'

'No, sir! I drank twenty-one pints in four hours. Here's a photograph of me doing it.'

He unearthed a luridly coloured snapshot of himself standing at a bar, crimson in the face, sweating and grinning with the tankard raised.

'I was ill for a fortnight afterwards,' he admitted.

On the day of the move, when the fridge was dragged clear of the kitchen wall, the dehydrated corpse of a rat was found to be lodged behind the motor.

Brownie was triumphant.

'What did I say? Look at it, sir! You and Monsieur Beausson thought I was seeing things. You thought I had DTs. But I was seeing straight – I was right all along! There's the rat to prove I was telling you the truth!'

It was characteristic of him to confess he had drunk twenty-one pints of beer at a sitting, and then assert that none of his senses had ever been affected by his abuse of alcohol. Naturally he was pleased to be vindicated. But he also wanted to retreat a step or two into his favourite shadows of ambiguity, from which he had allowed himself to be enticed. And as usual he could not let slip an opportunity to boast of his toughness.

*

Hereward's bank-balance was in a bad way while he waited to get into his house, in spite of subsidies from his family.

One morning he received a legalistic letter from his landlords at Windle Road, invoking the clause of his lease that enjoined re-decoration of the maisonette throughout before he left it.

He was stunned. He had not bargained for extra costs of

maybe a thousand pounds to have the job done professionally. He threw the letter at Brownie, whose response was the more stoical the more frantic his boss became.

'We'll have to set to ourselves, sir.'

Whereupon he stripped off his white jacket and painted from dawn to dusk for a fortnight, tireless and always cheery, assisted by Hereward and an old-age pensioner by the name of Steve, probably a companion of his drinking days, whom he persuaded to help in return for free meals.

The work was finished, dead-lines were met, and Hereward's bill amounted to some thirty pounds for materials.

'You were marvellous, Brownie. I don't know how to repay you. I saved your life, you say. Well, you've saved my bacon. And you managed it on nothing stronger than cups of tea.'

They removed into 32 Trafalgar Terrace, N.W.3.

The basement had been converted into a self-contained flat, which was quickly furnished and let. On the ground floor were the entrance passage leading to the stairs, a bed-sitting-room for a lodger, Brownie's bedroom at the back, and a bathroom tacked on in the two-storey addition: Brownie and the lodger were to share the bathroom. His kitchen, where he had his TV and easy chair, adjoined Hereward's combined sitting and dining-room on the first floor. On the second and top floor were Hereward's bedroom-study and his bathroom.

They had more space than they were accustomed to. The rooms were larger with generous windows and higher ceilings. The front ones looked across the wide road at the flowers and trees in the gardens opposite, and from the rear ones the hillock of Highgate crowned with a church spire was visible. The house faced south-east and north-west, so that the sun shone in morning and evening. And the light seemed to be brighter, and the air fresher and purer, than at Windle Road. The season was spring: birds sang with rustic rapture in the dusty littered greenery of Hampstead Heath.

'What do you think of it, Brownie?'

'Champion, sir!'

The cul-de-sac was about a hundred and fifty yards in length. On one side of number 32 it was residential, on the other were the shops as in a village. All the houses, including those turned into shops, and the pub on the corner, were of roughly the same Victorian-Edwardian date. A central alley connected Trafalgar Terrace with the mews that ran along behind Brownie's kitchen.

A lodger materialised. The rents now flowing into Hereward's coffers allayed his dread of penury – and of no longer being able to follow his calling. He settled down and resumed his routine: breakfast at seven, writing until one, lunch and the afternoon off, a walk, tea, more writing, seeing friends if possible, and an early bed. Every three or four weeks he spent a few days with his family at Watkins Hall. As a rule he did not bother about an annual holiday.

Such disciplined regularity seemed to be the sort of strait-jacket that Brownie needed. He rose at six forty-five, served breakfast and as it was being consumed gave Hereward's room a cat's lick and a promise, went shopping, cleaned the other rooms, cooked lunch, did more shopping in the afternoon and polished the brasses on the front door and gossiped with passers-by, switched on the telly at six, prepared and served supper, and then smoked and dozed in his easy chair until bed-time. At intervals he visited his daughter and son-in-law and grandchildren, usually when Hereward was away for weekends. Every year, in the second fortnight of August, he repaired to a Butlin's Holiday Camp.

He was too busy to get bored: soon he was not only doing the contractual minimum of cleaning for the male lodger, but valeting his clothes and running errands. To the pretty young female tenant of the basement flat he lent kitchen equipment, and he cooked titbits and washed up for her. Half the householders in the terrace entrusted him with keys of their properties: he was always having to hurry somewhere to let in a gas-man or walk a dog or accept a delivery or draw curtains to bamboozle burglars.

Hereward warned him not to repeat his mistake of making an impossible amount of work for himself.

'But I love it, sir. And I feel so fit! And I never could say no to peoples.'

While his life on the whole was sufficiently humdrum and monotonous not to fray his nerves, it did not lack the essential ingredient of variety. At Hereward's suggestion party-givers of his acquaintance tried Brownie out, and were predictably delighted. The telephone began to ring for Brownie almost as often as it did for his master, his diary was full of engagements, and once or twice a week he would leave the house at three or four o'clock and return at midnight, having produced more or less of a banquet. Thus he was kept on his toes as he described it – his culinary talents were exercised, his gastronomic snobbery was indulged, also his social snobbery, since he met all the nobs at his parties, and he reaped an abundant harvest of praise.

Incidentally, for Hereward, a special satisfaction was that Mrs White, the wife of the psychiatrist who had advised him to have no dealings with lame ducks, was amongst Brownie's more demanding clients.

In short the gamble was paying – literally. Brownie's low weekly wage was just adequate during bad patches without extra-mural dinners. But in a good patch he earned a small fortune in fees and tips over and above it – and his entire income was pocket-money considering he was boarded and fed. He was able to buy expensive presents for his family, invest in new suits and still put a bit aside.

His liquid assets were not draining away. Part of the secret of the success of Hereward's scheme was that Brownie was not boozing – apparently he was at last adhering to his resolutions. He retained certain habits he had formed in bars: for instance he swallowed his tea lukewarm and in a single draught from an enormous cup that held a pint, and measured his daily intake of tea in pints. He resorted to the substitute of fizzy lemonade, dozens of bottles of which he martialled regimentally within reach of his kitchen chair. And he could not altogether change his spots, that is to say his addictive personality: he started to eat too much, and similarly to smoke his pipe – in twenty-four hours he got through two ounces of the strongest tobacco on the market. But, suspect as his friendship with the landlord of the village pub might be, there was no evidence to suggest that Brownie was one of his better customers.

The other part of the secret was his happiness. He was personally succeeding where many had failed, he was winning general approval instead of disapproval, and working for an English or at any rate a Welsh gentleman in a gentleman's residence, and mixing with the gentry to his heart's content.

He whistled loudly and out of tune as he attended to his duties. He was so spontaneously happy that he omitted to affect an inability to whistle. Or he sang a snatch of the vulgar Black Watch version of *The Ball of Kirriemuir*: 'Five and twenty maidenheads / Lined up against a wall ...' If he and Hereward were in London on a Sunday afternoon he pinned a Do-Not-Disturb notice on the door of his kitchen.

'May I come in?'

'*Entrez, Monsieur.*'

He would be sitting somnolent in his chair, replete after

a gargantuan meal, enveloped in tobacco smoke, surrounded by lemonade bottles, watching a Western on his telly.

'Where are you, Brownie? I can scarcely see you for smoke. It's like a Turkish brothel in here.'

'Not much of a brothel, sir, without any goods for sale. All the same it's nice.'

*

Happiness is fattening. He became a jolly fat man with double chins and a belly that burst the relevant buttons on his shirts. He began to utter his complaint that modern clothes in the shops were made for queers, meaning persons thinner than he was. He would draw in his midriff and inflate his chest and flex his biceps and say his figure was too fine for the skimpy products of the rag trade.

At other times, if anyone criticised his girth, he would hold his breath until his eyes protruded alarmingly and his face turned purple, blow out his cheeks and thrust out his stomach, so that he looked like a gross apoplectic toad.

It was a joke, intended to show how little he cared.

But he was worried when he discovered he weighed nearly sixteen stones.

'You'll have to eat less, Brownie.'

'I've stopped drinking, sir. I can't stop eating. You'll want me to stop breathing next.'

He claimed he had heavy bones and was growing more muscular: 'I'm built on the lines of a bison.' He nonetheless went on a permanent diet, at least in theory. He would starve himself for a few days, or cut down to one daily meal instead of four, or resist bread and potatoes, or ration his pints of tea – and boast of his iron will.

But he was inclined to forget he was meant to be slimming. And the customs of his class were against him: he visited members of his family who expressed their affectionate feelings by stuffing him with great greasy cooked breakfasts, lunches on outsize plates, salmon salads and meat sandwiches at six o'clock, and a milky drink and a half-pound packet of Custard Cream biscuits before retiring. For that matter the nature of his work was no help: he had to taste, and no doubt he was tantalised beyond bearing by, the food he was employed to cook.

However, forgetfulness and extenuating circumstances apart, he again invested Hereward with an authority which he then seemed to be determined to flout. The thing he could never stop doing was to practise his deceptions.

'Brownie, what's become of the roast chicken we had for dinner the other evening?'

'You ate most of it, sir. And I had a morsel. And it was really a *poussin*, sir. I gave the carcase to a hungry old-age pensioner I know to make a bowl of broth with . . .'

'Brownie, why are you cooking so much stew?'

'I thought you might have guests, sir. And I'll be needing a saucer-full. You can't run a car without petrol. Well – I can't run myself ragged for you for about a hundred hours a week without any nourishment. Besides, whatever's left of the stew won't be wasted. It'll keep me going for four or five days . . .'

He exaggerated. His stews did not last so long. After twenty-four hours, when he had finished them, he would tell Hereward they had turned nasty. The saucer referred to belonged to his pint cup and was as big as a soup-plate.

Hereward, who liked his bread brown, would enquire: 'Why did I find a loaf of white bread hidden behind the glasses in the glass cupboard?'

'Is that where I put it? I was hunting for it all over. I'm so absent-minded! Thank you for finding it, sir. I bought it for your breadcrumbs. I wanted it to get stale enough to grate into breadcrumbs.'

'But it's only a bit of a loaf.'

'I cut the crusts off, sir, so it would get stale quicker.'

'But each of the crusts must have been a quarter of the loaf.'

'Oh no, sir. The baker told me it was a new shape. The crusts I cut were no thicker than shavings.'

'What did you do with them?'

'I chucked them out for a sparrow. I didn't eat them, if that's what you're thinking, sir. I'm on my diet, remember – which wouldn't permit me.'

Sometimes he played the game in a different way.

On being asked what he had done with crusts of forbidden bread he replied defiantly: 'I scoffed them with oodles of dripping!'

Hereward would laugh and comment: 'Well, it's your own look-out. I'd far rather you were fat than drunk. But I understood you were dead-set on losing weight. All I can say is you won't on bread and dripping.'

Brownie's defence of his lapses in this context included the taunt that he consoled himself with food because he was not allowed to consort with women.

'But you are, Brownie! I wish you did more consorting. You'd be less lonely and less likely to be tempted back into pubs. Why not marry again?'

'No, thanks, sir – I've been bitten!'

'You could consort without marrying. You've got your room downstairs. What goes on in it is your business.'

'Let a female foot in the door? Never, sir! There'd be hell to pay.'

92

'Consort elsewhere in that case. Take a woman to a cinema or a theatre. You can have as much free time as you like.'

'What about my work, sir? You've no idea how hard I have to work to keep you straight.'

'Nonsense, Brownie! You spend hours smoking in your kitchen chair. You might just as well be enjoying yourself with a member of the opposite sex. In my opinion it'd do you good.'

Hereward meant it. He was vaguely concerned by Brownie's reluctance to project the normalisation of his existence into normal social, not to mention sexual, inter-course. He guessed that a subsidiary bad habit of Brownie's was not to mix with people except in the street, in shops and particularly in pubs. He hoped that Brownie was now afraid of being pressed to have a quick one by hospitable friends and acquaintances. A sensible middle-aged maternal type would keep him safely and soberly under her wing and be company for him.

But Brownie was adamant. He refused invitations even to have a cup of coffee in another house. And he never returned to see his cronies in the Windle Road area – maybe because he had left unpaid debts behind him.

As for the question of women, Hereward was discomforted later on by his naïve attempts to answer it.

Brownie's alcoholic preoccupations had been exclusive – and blurred every issue for ten years. Divorced, uninspired by drink, older and fatter, he seemed to lack libidinous initiative and self-confidence. He over-ate, he said his kitchen on a Sun-day afternoon was not much of a brothel, and put the blame on his boss.

Hereward might have saved himself the trouble of encour-aging Brownie, whose sex-appeal was at once magnetic and perennial. He could seduce any woman of any age and description in one way or another. He was therefore in a position to pick and choose – and if and when he felt like doing so, he chose not a middle-aged maternal type but the most nubile piece of grummet available.

At the same time he knew the score. He had had the lesson dinned into him not merely by his wife. By temperament he was too flirtatious and provocative, too fickle, and too vulnerable for the war of the sexes. He was cynical about women – he derided them, he dreaded their inevitable reproaches, as only a male chauvinist who has often been loved and hated can.

In principle – and in the meanwhile – he preferred his plaintive celibacy and to stay at home.

*

But there was always a gap between his principles and his practice. He could not help meeting women in the terrace. He showered terms of endearment on them indiscriminately: each was his sweetheart, his princess, his passion-flower, his luscious lump of Turkish delight, and more rudely his Polo Mint.

He would shout out to an old crock shuffling past in her bedroom slippers: 'How's your love-life, darling?'

His naughty jokes were rejuvenating. He could make even the sourest puss laugh. Almost every morning Hereward's writing was disturbed by shrieks of laughter from the street below. Brownie would be ringed round by a group of stout aggressive housewives, throwing back their heads and guffawing. He was so chatty, comical, quick at repartee and scandalously vulgar: married as no doubt they were to average dull prim husbands, it was not surprising that they fell for him. He offered to do their washing along with his own in the village launderette: 'My pants and your knickers could have a mad whirl together in the soapsuds.' He told them about a *budgeregard* – a budgerigar – and how it utilised the red-topped match it was given to play with. He went far too far, debunked, teased, and swapped recipes and insults.

'Never, Mr Brown! . . . Get away with you . . . None of your cheek now . . . You foul devil you!'

He fought their verbal battles with shopkeepers, who were terrified of his uninhibited tongue and talent for ridicule. He carried their shopping-bags and listened to their troubles and sympathised and cheered them up. He lent them money.

A pretty antique-dealer opened a shop in the terrace. Brownie developed a sudden interest in antiques. She resisted his light-hearted overtures. He had his revenge by spreading the story that she was a lesbian. Then she refused to speak to him. But one morning she called at number 32 and handed over ten pounds to Hereward.

She explained: 'I arrived at work the other day without my purse. I was desperate, in a rush, and didn't know where to turn. So I asked Brownie for a tenner. He's a dirty old man and a frightful liar. All the same I'm fond of him. And there's nobody else I would have liked to borrow from.'

He was generous – and receptive and unshockable – and the repository of secrets.

A girl in a flat across the terrace was deserted by her husband. She confessed to Brownie that she was being driven demented by the loss of her conjugal rights. She began to pester him with propositions.

Hereward suggested: 'Well, why not?'

'I can't fancy it.'

'The proverb says: don't look a gift-horse in the mouth.'

'She lives too close, sir. And another proverb says: don't mess in your own nest.'

A prerequisite of what he fancied was a sturdy pair of legs. 'I only go for girls with legs strong enough to crack a man like a nut.'

In spite of his ban on girls who lived too close, he did some consorting with a temporary neighbour named Maureen. The fact that Maureen was at least an amateur prostitute minimised his fear of involvement. After her departure he showed Hereward a photograph taken in her bed-sitting-room by a third party. In it he was fully dressed in his gentleman's gentleman's togs, dignified dark suit and overcoat and Homburg hat to match, and carried his rolled umbrella. But the umbrella in his right hand was raised as if to challenge the photographer to a duel, on his face was an expression of demonic glee, and his left hand was up Maureen's skirt.

There were a couple of real pros in the terrace, a mother and daughter, who apparently paid for everything with their favours, groceries, minicab rides. Brownie thought they were the accomplices of burglars and gave them the widest possible berth.

Once the harridan of a mother started to ask him leading questions.

'Why do you wear a white jacket? What do you and that tall fellow do for a living? What's your line of business?'

'We're abortionists,' he replied.

He got away with saying unforgivable things. He was always skirmishing with the Jewish family that ran the shop where he bought his tobacco. The wife of the proprietor attempted habitually, if in vain, to short-change him, he said. He concluded one of their public slanging-matches with the rhetorical exclamation: 'Why did Hitler let the ovens out?' Hereward was horrified when he was told about it. But Mrs

Rosenberg reacted more in a Christian than a Jewish spirit. Turning the other cheek, she and her husband continued to sell Brownie his tobacco and laugh at his callous racialist sallies.

He did not reserve his offensive remarks which never seemed to offend for the weaker sex. He was friendly with a huge coal-black painter and decorator, Johnny Mgubba, who frequented the pub in the terrace. Johnny was apt to get drunk and to swagger up and down the street, beating his breast and bellowing: 'I am the Chief of all the Mgubbas!'

Brownie would greet him: 'Hullo, Johnny-boy! How's your health today? You're looking as white as a sheet.'

Before a General Election Brownie obliged Hereward by sticking a Conservative Party poster in a window.

Johnny Mgubba, who was passing, noticed and called: 'Hey! What are you doing? You're not Conservative.'

'That's right,' Brownie agreed non-committally.

'What's your politics then?'

'I support Enoch Powell.'

He was no respecter of persons, female, male, white, black, little, large, humble, grand – although superficially he could adapt like a chameleon to the class and susceptibilities of his companions. He was vulgar with the vulgar, common with commoners, refined with the refined, posh with the upper crust, and so on. But sooner or later he prevailed upon most people to rise or stoop to his basic level.

He laid siege to the daily cleaner from next door. She was in her fifties, married, respectable, even forbidding. He showed her snapshots of his grandchildren. They got on to Christian name terms. He began to escort her to her bus-stop in the afternoons.

One afternoon, as he assisted her into a crowded bus, he

blew her a kiss and asked: 'Which night is it your husband's working, dear?' – so that everyone could hear.

On another afternoon he shouted after her: 'I never will believe it's my baby!'

The local chemist, a pal of his, employed an attractive bashful sixteen-year-old girl to serve his customers.

Brownie entered the shop and approached the counter.

'Oh – miss – I wonder – could I have a word with Mr Carter, please?' he enquired in a nervous tone of voice.

But Mr Carter had been briefed beforehand: mixing medicines behind a screen, he said he was occupied.

'Well, miss – it's like this, miss – I'm sure I don't know how to put it – I've never had much to do with ladies, miss – but my girlfriend's parents are on holiday and she's invited me to her place this evening and I don't want to get her in trouble – not the very first time, miss. Can you help me? Do you think – well – I ought to have something – take something with me – I mean just in case? Perhaps one of those things to wear – what are they called? And what size, miss?'

The wretched girl, having almost died of embarrassment, was revived by Brownie's involuntary laughter at his last question, in which Mr Carter, and she herself eventually, joined.

*

He had more fun and games in the houses where he cooked dinners, mainly with the maids, nannies, baby-sitters and au-pair girls who gave him a hand.

That could actually happen.

'Were you working on your own at the Lockett's?'

'No, sir. Their au-pair was with me in the kitchen.'

'What's she like?'

'Saucy, sir – we held hands in the washing-up water.'

He talked a lot about the capabilities and competence of a nanny in a certain house. Hereward's impression was that she must be the usual kindly old retainer. But then Brownie mentioned kisses.

'What sort of evening did you have?'

'Not bad – I got a kiss or two out of it.'

'Who kissed you?'

'Nanny, sir.'

'Really? And you and she kissed more than once?'

'Oh yes, sir.'

'I don't think I quite understand. Were these kisses pecks on the cheek?'

'No, sir – not pecks – proper knee-tremblers.'

He called proper or improper kisses either knee-tremblers or kilt-lifters.

'But, Brownie, what age is Nanny, for heaven's sake?'

'Eighteen, sir. She's a beautiful blonde with a figure like Marilyn Monroe.'

Hereward often warned Brownie not to practise his wiles on the youth and innocence of the girls he met in strange kitchens.

'The baby-sitter last night was a tasty bit of crackling.'

'I hope you didn't have a nibble.'

'Sir! She's younger than my daughter, sir! She's just a child.'

'That's what worries me. I don't trust you with female children.'

'They've all got to learn, haven't they?'

'Maybe – but not all of them necessarily from you.'

Sometimes one or other of the girls he had flirted with rang him up to propose that they should carry on in their spare time. He was disconcerted, and would protest coldly that none of his time was spare.

Once a client telephoned about her Fijian maid, who was sinking into a deep depression for unrequited love of Brownie.

'What did you do to her?'

'Nothing, sir.'

'I bet you led her up the garden path.'

But he was unrepentant.

He assumed that hackneyed hypocritical masculine attitude which is the strongest argument against permissiveness: 'Well – she didn't ought to have let herself be led.'

As a rule he succeeded in locking love out: his lust was so ruthlessly irresponsible. A former lodger in the room on the ground floor invited Brownie to his wedding. For a change he accepted, went along, kissed the bride, drank a glass of champagne to toast the happy pair, and ended by spending the night with a fellow-guest.

'She was full of the joys of spring. Women are pushovers after weddings.'

'Will you see her again?'

'I doubt it, sir.'

'Why not?'

'I'm not that keen.'

'Won't she want to see you?'

'I gave her the wrong telephone number.'

On holiday at a Butlin's Camp a girl he nicknamed Peanut became his partner for dancing etcetera. Evidently he was an expert dancer, rhythmical and light-footed, notwithstanding his bulk. He disengaged from Peanut by promising to meet her at the same time in the same place the following year – and promptly booked in at a different camp.

With the mistresses of the houses where he cooked he again had fun, if not the games he played with their staff. The titled ones he addressed as 'My lady' instead of 'Milady', and all those without titles as 'Madame' instead of 'Madam'. To the husband of a titled wife he would refer to her as 'Our lady', probably meaning to crack a sacrilegious joke although he kept a straight face. His eccentricities and absurdities were a part of the entertainment he was paid to provide.

'Can I press you to a Brussels sprout, Madame? . . . You must get outside another dollop of my mousse, dear sir!'

Meanwhile he gathered material for the book he planned to write about the bad manners and peculiar habits of his so-called superiors. Some of his clients tried to diddle him: for instance he would quote a price for a dinner for four and find he was expected to prepare cocktail snacks for twenty without any extra fee. Some were stingy: they would economise on food for him to eat, or want to know what he had done with the watery dregs of Dry Martini in the cocktail shaker, or haggle over his bus-fares. A woman who should have known better required him to quarrel telephonically with her grocer for refusing to deliver an order of a packet of salt at six o'clock in the evening. Another, more scatter-brained, would ask him to follow an abstruse recipe, hoover her sitting-room, fool around with her children and zip up the back of her dress simultaneously.

The hosts at these parties were liable to tempt him with drinks. The story he told Hereward was that he explained frankly and fully why he did not dare so much as sniff alcohol. He was resentful of a malicious gentleman who nonetheless forced him to taste every bottle of wine before serving it.

And he had his enemies amongst party-goers: a literary lion who sat sideways at dinner tables, impeding Brownie's laborious progress with platters, and a thoughtless professor who helped himself to more than his share of meals and made it look as if Brownie had got his quantities wrong.

In one house he had an enemy in the shape of a ferocious bull-terrier. Moreover its owner and his clients were hard-working people – they gave him a key with which to gain admittance before they returned from their offices. When he first tried to do so he was bitten by their dog, waiting for him on the other side of the front door. His strategy on that and future occasions was ingenious as ever. He retreated, bought a supply of Mars Bars, pushed them through the letter-box, and while they were being masticated slipped in.

But on the whole he not only loved or at any rate was stimulated by his excursions into a world of fashion, and the representatives, the paraphernalia, the opulence and glamour of the social establishment – he was loved, even in the end by savage greedy dogs, and valued and treated well.

His particular favourite was Mrs Pemberton-Wicklow, a merry widow, a relentless hostess, and physically a heavy-weight. She reciprocated his feelings: once on an unconventional impulse she embraced him.

'Was it enjoyable?'

'Yes and no, sir. She half-squeezed the life out of me. She's like a boa-constrictor.'

'Did you do any constricting?'

'I always do my bit, sir. No – seriously – I'll tell you what it was like. You know the advertisement on TV with a boy and a girl running towards each other in slow motion through a misty cornfield? I ran into Mrs Pemberton-Wicklow's arms and she ran into mine like that.'

*

After Hereward's father's death, his mother continued to live in a few of the rooms of the ancestral home, attended by her equally ageing Welsh housekeeper Mrs Williams. When Mrs Williams went on holiday, Brownie replaced her. And he began to accompany his boss to Watkins Hall to help with the work at weekends and at Christmas.

He soon won Mrs Williams over, in spite of her bucolic hostility to a smart operator from the metropolis. He said he was partly Scottish – Celtic as she was; and he brought her peace offerings, false jewellery and a pair of yellow satin knickers with a butterfly embroidered on the front. Screams of unwonted laughter issued from the kitchen.

One day Mrs Williams remarked to Hereward: 'Now you'll be ready for a quiet time down here, considering you're so busy in London.'

'I haven't been especially busy since I finished my last book,' he replied.

'I mean with the people you have in to lunch and dinner.'

'But I seldom have people in. Where did you get hold of that idea?'

'Your Brownie told me he was cooking for ten or twelve for every meal.'

'I'm afraid you can't believe a word he says.'

'Oh I don't,' Mrs Williams agreed hurriedly, mortified at having fallen into the trap of alien urban deceitfulness after all.

Back in Trafalgar Terrace, Hereward was chatting to a neighbour.

It was in the spring; and he volunteered the information that he had recently visited his mother; whereupon he was asked: 'Did you have good sport? Shoot any grouse?'

'Grouse? No! I shouldn't think there's a grouse within hundreds of miles of the Brecon Beacons. And I stopped shooting ages ago – and anyway it's the wrong time of year for shooting grouse.'

'Oh – I'm sorry – I understood you had a grouse moor in the grounds of the castle.'

'What castle?'

'Where your mother lives – Watkins Castle.'

'Actually it's called Watkins Hall – and it's a medium-sized manor house with a ruined Victorian wing. I suppose you've been listening to Brownie's fairy tales?'

'Well, yes – he said it had turrets and a flag-pole for the family standard and a drawbridge.'

'Did he indeed?'

'And he likes being there because of the flighty red-headed French lady's maid.'

'What did he have to say about the grounds?'

'I got the impression you owned most of South Wales.'

Hereward confronted Brownie with his lies. But he realised that reform in this area was out of the question: in the first place Brownie could scarcely open his mouth without *proverbing* the truth, or at least exaggerating – and in the second an inherent class difference between them would never be erased. For Brownie's shamefully poor origins urged the widest possible publication of his present relative affluence and the other advantages he had wrested from the tight fist of fortune; whereas Hereward's wealthy aristocratic ones urged him in the opposite direction – towards playing down the privileges of his birth and understatement of his subsequent success or good luck.

'You've been at it again, Brownie – making out my mother queens it in a castle and I shoot grouse in her garden. I don't mind you boasting about yourself. But I won't have you misrepresenting me as a bloated plutocrat. Now I know why everything I buy in the terrace is so pricey. The shopkeepers must think I'm a millionaire – and a mean millionaire at that. You'll spread Communism.'

'I am a Communist, sir,' he retorted with his shifty giggle.

'Don't be silly! Since you were a boy of fourteen you've been dependent on Capitalism, financially, psychologically. If you don't vote Conservative you're just a humbug.'

'Yes, sir – that's what we Communists are, sir.'

He was teasing. But he was also resisting pressure to change his ways. He was too fond of basking in the imaginary glory he bestowed on his boss.

'You'll get me strung up to the nearest lamp-post when the revolution comes.'

'Have no fear, sir – Brownie's here!'

In fact, politically, he was on the extreme right. He loathed Bolshies and believed they were to blame for all our national ills. He advocated the control of mob violence with flame-throwers.

And his rhyming catch-phrase – 'Have no fear, Brownie's here!' – had an element of truth in it. He at once slandered Hereward – 'I have to empty his ashtray after every cigarette he smokes ... I have to get on my knees to pull his muddy boots off ... He can't do nothing for himself ... One day he boiled an egg for an hour and wondered why the shell didn't go soft' – and protected him. He slept with a length of lead pipe under his pillow and gave instruction in the art of dealing with an intruder.

'Suppose a villain rings the doorbell in the middle of the night, or more likely in the middle of the afternoon, what do you do?'

'I tell you to answer it.'

'Thank you, sir. All right – provided I'm at home I tickle him with my blunt instrument. But suppose I'm not at home, what's your procedure?'

'I look out of the window to see who's there – and don't let him in.'

'But you won't know he's a villain however hard you look at him. He won't be wearing a black mask and carrying a sack over his shoulder. He'll be in a natty suit – and he'll say he's from the Council, or he's collecting money for nuns. Suppose he talks you downstairs, how do you open the front door?'

'Like this?'

'No, sir. You should step backwards when you open the door, so you've got room to kick him in the crutch when he rushes you. And where are you going to hit him?'

'But I've already kicked him, I've probably crippled him – must I hit him as well?'

'Definitely! Aim for his throat, chop him across the throat and block his windpipe, or blind him by sticking your thumb in his eye. And kick him again when you've got him on the floor.'

'Do I send for the police after I've finished with him, or an ambulance?'

'You should be able to send for the undertaker, sir.'

Brownie was specially protective of Hereward's bank-balance. He was a virtuoso of a shopper, carrying in his head and comparing the prices of almost every article in a number of shops, and thinking nothing of walking half a mile to save a few pence. He shamed profiteering shopkeepers, and got things cheap either because he intimidated them with his wit, or because his custom and goodwill were worth culti-vation, or because he had spun some heart-breaking yarn.

He would tell a butcher he wanted to treat a starving arthritic pensioner to a square meal and bring back a bargain mixed grill for supper. He had no scruples about begging a bite to eat for his invalid father.

'I'll have a nice leg of lamb for my boss – and do me a favour and throw in a handful of scrag-end for my father.'

At length the local butcher enquired suspiciously: 'Just how old and sick is this father of yours?'

Brownie's answer, whatever it was, must have implicated Hereward, who was shaken when another shopkeeper said to him with a sly smile a day or two later: 'I'm glad you're feeling better, sir.'

*

Hereward liked none of the public roles in which he seemed to have been cast – millionaire, miser, tyrant, spoilt brat, and ailing father of a sort of confidence trickster who was his senior by thirteen years.

He felt he was being stared at by strangers as he walked down the street. He found it a particular strain to be abroad in his manservant's company. He was uneasily aware that together they bore a comic resemblance to Don Quixote and Sancho Panza. And Brownie was irrepressible and adept at causing embarrassment for a joke: witness the incident with the girl in the chemist's shop.

Once Hereward was commiserating with an octogenarian lady in a wheelchair when Brownie hailed her: 'How are the bowels, passion-flower?'

Again, they stopped to pass the time of day with some scaffolders who were working on the house next door. But after a few minutes Hereward had to hurry away. Brownie's quips on the theme of scaffold-poles and nuts and bolts were too crude to listen to.

Punctuality was his God. He would rebuke artisans who failed to arrive on time in the mornings: 'I know, I know – you lay too long in bed with your hand on your brains ...' A corpulent official of the Gas Board, who was near retiring age, clocked in the regular couple of hours late for an appointment. Brownie said: 'Where have you been hiding, matey? Why can't you leave your missis alone – and do your work instead? I'll give you a piece of free advice: put it on the window-sill and bang the window on it . . .'

Hereward bought a car which he parked in his front garden. Other drivers were apt to block his exit with their vehicles. On one occasion Brownie caught a person at it.

In front of Hereward he shouted: 'Clear off! We're a team of brain surgeons, waiting for an emergency call. If you park there and stop us driving out, the patient could die. And we'd have you up for manslaughter.'

He also warned would-be parkers in the wrong place: 'Want me to run a six-inch nail along your paintwork? Want me to light a bonfire under your petrol tank?'

He was fearless, at any rate in speech, although he usually modified his aggressive remarks to members of his own sex by adding the word sir, even in conversation with the most oafish youth.

He was motoring somewhere with Hereward. They pulled in at a transport cafe, entered the shack of a building which was full of lorry drivers, sat on high stools at the messy counter and studied the gravy-stained menu. A lumbering negro came to take their order.

Brownie gave it: 'Fried egg and fried bread, bacon, sausage and tomato twice, if you'd be so kind.'

He continued in his fancy voice: 'And this gentleman here likes his fried bread golden brown, and his eggs hard on the bottom and soft on top, with a nice crisp frilly edge – sir!'

The negro rolled his eyes and Hereward blushed.

On another day in a supermarket they were standing in a queue at the pay-desk behind a shopper in a fur coat.

'Beg pardon, Madame,' Brownie addressed her: 'but I wonder if you've heard what they say about ladies in beautiful coats like yours?'

Luckily she laughed and lifted the hem of the coat to show she had clothes on underneath.

Brownie's affectations were a measure of how far he was prepared to go in search of amusement – his own, if no one else's.

He started to limp round Hereward's dining-table one evening.

A sympathetic guest asked him what was wrong.

'It's my foot, sir.'

'What have you done to your foot?'

'It happened in the war, sir. A German tank ran over my instep.'

'Oh dear – I'm sorry. But what a miracle you've got any foot left!'

'The terrain was muddy. I sort of sank into it. But my toes have never been the same.'

'I should think not!'

'I can't touch the ground with them. They will stick up in the air. Look, sir.'

And he exhibited his foot with the toecap of his shoe pointing upwards.

'That must be terribly uncomfortable.'

'It is, sir. But the doctors can't help me. I just have to make the best of it.'

Hereward intervened to say: 'Funny that I've never noticed anything the matter with your foot.'

'I'm a bit shy about it, sir. I've always tried to conceal it.'

'Let's see you walk, Brownie.'

He hobbled a few paces.

'But you don't walk like that normally.'

'I'm afraid the trouble's getting worse, sir.'

Later, alone with Brownie, Hereward expressed his scepticism more forcibly.

'May you be forgiven!'

'I shall be, sir. I'm telling the sober truth.'

To prove his point he hobbled everywhere within the house and in its immediate vicinity for several weeks, toecap vertical.

He was ready to suffer for his affectations. He pretended he could not – or rather refused to – regulate his intake of medicines, wishing to suggest he was too tough to be either healed or hurt by them. As a result he repeatedly poisoned himself.

'You haven't been drinking, Brownie?'

'Never, sir! But yesterday I went to consult my doctor about my wonky shoulder. And now I keep on seeing stars – it's as bad as being on the booze.'

'What did your doctor do for you?'

'He wrote out a prescription for tablets.'

'Have you started taking them?'

'Started and stopped, sir.'

'You don't mean you've taken all the tablets?'

'Yes, sir.'

'Where's the bottle? But it says here – one at night. How many tablets did you take?'

'I lost count. I swilled them down with a pint of tea – they were such tiny tots. And I never can be bothered with one at a time.'

'Well – you're a lunatic.'

'Maybe, sir. But I've given my wonky shoulder a fright. It hasn't dared to pain me since.'

He was stubbornly affected. He was affected even in adversity.

He was advised by his dentist, who had pulled out half a dozen of his teeth under a general anaesthetic, to rinse his mouth.

He was scarcely conscious, and his mouth was probably awash with blood.

But he replied: 'Sorry, sir – I don't think I will – because I'd have to swallow what I rinsed with – you see, sir, I can't spit.'

*

Towards the end of his long happy period at Trafalgar Terrace two incidents occurred which he described to Hereward – and Hereward then dined out on.

Brownie in his boss's absence received an unusual visitor at number 32.

'He was a plain-clothes police officer, sir – a charming gentleman. He said there might be a housebreaker holed up in the mews, and wanted to have a peep from our back windows. I told him a housebreaker would never be able to afford the rent of any house round here. But anyway I let him in – he showed me his identity card. I hope I did right.'

A week later Hereward returned home at about midnight. Brownie in an excited state was waiting for him.

'They've caught Cat's-eyes, sir!'

'Who's Cat's-eyes?'

'Cat's-eyes Callaghan, the bank robber! The police arrested him. And I saw the whole thing!'

'What happened?'

'I was cooking my supper. I was cooking my pound of chipolatas when the doorbell rang. The officer who called the other day asked if he could position two of his men in the yard behind our basement flat. I gave permission – and hurried back to my kitchen and put my chipolatas on a plate and the plate and the mustard-pot on the draining-board by the window and switched off the light. The terrace was crammed with police-cars and constables – but everything seemed to be quiet round about the mews. A voice boomed through one of those loud-hailers. The next minute I thought I heard a door slam – actually it was a skylight being thrown wide open – and some glass broke. And somebody was running across the flat roof of the mews house opposite – he was just like a shadow although he was only ten yards from where I was watching. He got to the middle of the roof and the policemen in our basement yard shone their torches on him. He stopped. He was dressed all in black with a black beard. You could see he knew he was done for. But he ran on and jumped down from the roof of the last house in the mews. He jumped right into the arms of a posse of police.'

'What a thrill, Brownie!'

'It was, sir. I was leaning on the draining-board and dipping my chipolatas in the mustard-pot – I burnt my gullet to a crisp with mustard. But it was better than the telly.'

'Did you talk to the officer in charge afterwards?'

'Yes, sir. I said I couldn't help feeling sorry for Cat's-eyes when he stopped in the beams of the torches. He told me not to waste my pity on a nasty piece of work. And he laughed at my idea that the criminal he was chasing couldn't afford much of a rent. Cat's-eyes had twenty thousand pounds on him in a money-belt.'

'How long had he lived in the mews?'

'Six months, I believe.'

'Didn't you come across him?'

'No, sir. He was hiding and never set foot in the terrace by day. But he spoke to shopkeepers on the telephone. Every week he ordered a dozen bottles of vodka from the off-licence and a case of avocado pears from the greengrocer.'

'Nothing else?'

'No, sir.'

'Not a very healthy diet.'

'No.'

'Twelve bottles of vodka a week can't have done him much good.'

'I agree, sir,' Brownie replied smugly.

The other incident also involved the police.

Again Hereward was absent on the afternoon in question. Brownie was wiping over the floor of the hall when he heard a key turning in the lock of the front door. He opened the door – he imagined his boss was trying to get in. An insignificant weaselly tramp was standing outside.

The following exchange took place.

'Who are you? What do you think you're doing?'

'I was using this here key you give me.'

'What? What key?'

'This here key you give me in Wormwood Scrubs.'

'I didn't give you any key in Wormwood Scrubs! I've never been in Wormwood Scrubs! You were going to burgle my house, weren't you?'

'Yuss!'

'Get out of it!'

And Brownie administered a push that sent the fellow reeling backwards: he did not need to kick him in the crutch or chop him across the throat or blind him.

He pushed and pursued, banging the door shut, and asked a passing neighbour to ring the police without delay. The ineffective intruder was now slumped on the kerb of the pavement, speechless and with his head in his hands. Brownie stood over him, guarding him unnecessarily, and fuming on account of the allegation that he was a party to the planned theft.

Sirens wailed, and a police-car with flashing blue lamp, two policemen on motorcycles, a van containing four Alsatians and their handlers, and a Black Maria rolled up: 'An army arrived to arrest a shrimp!'

The shrimp was bundled into the Black Maria. Brownie was driven in the police-car to and from the police station, where he made and signed his statement.

On returning to the terrace he realised he had locked himself out of number 32. The door was shut and he did not have his own legitimate key in his pocket. As usual he seized his opportunity. He warned off other burglars by broadcasting the fact that he could not possibly force an entry.

'That place of ours is like a fortress!'

Eventually Hereward appeared on the scene, admitted him and was regaled with the story.

Brownie was duly summoned to speak his piece at a magistrate's court. In the witness-box he managed to create a mild sensation.

'Mr Brown, were you in Wormwood Scrubs Prison with the accused?'

'No, sir.'

'Were you ever in Wormwood Scrubs Prison?'

'No, sir.'

'Were you ever in prison anywhere?'

'Yes, sir.'

'What was that?'

'I said yes, sir – sir!'

'Please think carefully before you answer my next question, Mr Brown. Would you inform this court where exactly, when, and for what offence or offences you were imprisoned?'

'Germany – between 1940 and 1941 and again between 1944 and 1945 – for fighting for my king and country – SAH!'

5

Hereward Watkins was a generous friend. He often invited me round to meals at Trafalgar Terrace. With the royalties from his books, his rents and private income, he was richer than me. But that is not saying much – he was still worried about money. And wealth, whether relative or absolute, is by no means a synonym for hospitality.

Hereward was generous and Brownie always warmly welcoming.

'What a treat to see you again, dear sir.'

'No, it's my treat, Brownie. How are you?'

'Fit as a flea, thank you, sir. And yourself?'

'Oh, not too bad.'

'That's the ticket!'

The mere sight of his round rosy cheeks and comfortable corporation under his white jacket put an instant edge on my appetite. His confidence and optimism banished dull dyspeptic care. His relaxed conviviality was conducive to over-eating. His own greed, far from disgusting, was infectious.

Even a slab of Cheddar cheese served by Brownie seemed to taste better than cheese anywhere else. It was presented so temptingly: 'This is a crumbly mature strong Cheddar, sir – it'll blow your head off – it's more-ish!'

At Trafalgar Terrace he confined himself to cooking the sort of food most men prefer: grills with chips and roasts with roast potatoes, stews, eggs and paper-thin streaky bacon, crinkly and crisp, savouries of sardines or soft roes on toast. He was mad on fish: he said he would have cut his mother's throat for a wing of skate: which must have been why his breadcrumbed fillets of plaice were unparalleled.

He would carry a couple of tray-tables into the sitting-room, so that Hereward and I could eat in the armchairs by the fire and watch the telly. But he was more amusing than the majority of programmes.

'What's the gossip, Brownie?'

He might hark back to the Piccadilly Club or his wartime experiences. He might dance for us – just a step or two – suddenly loose-limbed and extraordinarily expressive – also graceful, if a trifle grotesque. He might mention somebody in the terrace and imitate the way that he or she walked – 'You know him, sir, he walks like this!' He had a unique gift for imitating walks – and was as merciless as the best comedians: he could do cripples to perfection. Or he might expatiate on the subject of lodgers.

For instance that Mr Carstairs, who lodged in the ground floor front room for some months, had a weekend wife in the country and a mistress in town. For the sake of appearances he would sneak into number 32 at half-past seven in the morning, undress, put on pyjamas, get into bed, and yawn and stretch and pretend he had just woken up when Brownie called him at eight.

Another lodger was a refugee from Bulgaria. He had anglicised his name to Smith and was a door-to-door salesman of encyclopedias. Brownie discovered that Mr Smith had been born a prince and never failed to refer to him as His Royal Highness.

'His Royal Highness gave me no end of trouble – he was a messy young pup.'

A married couple moved into the room. The husband was a martinet, the wife a martyr in Brownie's eyes. One day their car broke down. He sat in the driving seat and expected her to provide the motive power to get it started. And he encouraged her by yelling through the window : 'Push, you cow !'

'What else, Brownie ?'

'The worst was Mr Boyd in the basement flat. He was a sex maniac. He came home with a different woman every evening. He used to chase them something wicked, singing *Jerusalem* at the top of his voice.'

'Did he catch them ?'

'He must have, sir. Once he asked me to change his sheets. I needed a hammer.'

If Hereward had invited other people to a meal, we ate at the dining-table in a corner of the room. The ladies present invariably asked Brownie for his recipes. He would describe the speed or intensity at which he boiled liquids by reproducing the sound of the process.

'You bring the mixture to boiling-point, Madame – bllop, bllop ! Then you boil it a bit faster – bllop-bllop, bllop-bllop ! And before you pour it you step on the gas – bllop bllop bllop bllop bllop !'

He made lemon barley-water in the summer. It was wonderfully cool and refreshing, and sweet and sharp and bland. Even guests unaccustomed to non-alcoholic drinks consumed gallons of it. He wrote out that recipe repeatedly.

'Oh, Brownie, how good of you ! Now I'll be able to have delicious barley-water for all my parties. Thank you so much !'

Of course he had omitted an essential ingredient.

Disappointed hostesses would interrogate him about their

failures, his ready explanations of which confounded confusion: 'Are you sure you blanched your lemons, Madame? Are you sure you used the pus of the fruit? It wouldn't taste nice without the full flavour of pus.'

But sooner or later most of his victims saw the joke.

'You brute, Brownie! I've spent hours – days! – toiling over your fake recipe for barley-water. You fooled me completely! How could you? I kept on giving it to my husband, who thought I was trying to poison him.'

Hereward as host would remark ruefully that he was in the wrong place: he ought to be in the kitchen, and Brownie presiding at the head of the table.

'People enjoy talking to him more than talking to me. I don't blame them. I'd rather talk to him, too.'

In my view and in my memory they were complementary – Hereward aristocratic, pale and thin and attenuated, dignified, highbrow, accurate, preoccupied and on the melancholic side, and Brownie foreshortened, tubby, unbuttoned, bursting out all over, as common as muck in his own estimation, although in another sense exceptional, lowest-browed, whimsical, on the spot and always potentially manic. In music hall terms they were like a double act – the feed and the funster.

They both followed departing guests downstairs to the front door.

'Goodbye, Hereward – and thanks. Goodbye, Brownie.'

'Goodbye, sir.'

'Your dinner was pure poetry.'

'What did you think of my *Oeufs Trafalgar*?'

'Scrumptious! I meant to ask you: how are they done?'

'They're my invention, sir. They're simplicity itself. You soft-boil your *oeuf* and shell it under cold running water, and pop it in an individual *pot* and cover it with a loo-warm aspic mixture' – loo-warm equalled lukewarm in his phraseology. 'And then you drop slices of radish and chopped chives into the aspic before it sets, and serve out of the fridge.'

Hereward interposed: 'Is that the whole truth and nothing but the truth, Brownie?'

'Cross my heart, sir!'

'Your heart must be tired of getting crossed,' Hereward remarked.

'My heart's as sound as a dinner-bell – or it was until I started to work for you.'

The backchat and the laughter continued on the doorstep.

'Well – I really should be off.'

'Come again, sir.'

'I will if your boss invites me.'

'I'll see he does, sir.'

Walking or driving into the night, turning to wave by the alley into the mews, I used to feel I was leaving behind me an island of peace, order, compatibility and cosiness, amidst the turbulent seas of normal existence.

*

But an adage survives from the past in which the so-called leisured classes could find domestic staff to be served by – and to make a study of and draw conclusions from.

The ominous generalisation runs: 'Seven years a servant, seven years a friend, seven years a master.'

Brownie, not counting the period at Windle Road when he was employed by Jacques Beausson, had now been with Hereward for fifteen years.

The sun – and the stars – still shone on the island in Trafalgar Terrace.

Hereward's brave or reckless gamble on Brownie's sobriety

120

had turned out to be his best investment. Apart from the obvious dividends paid, it had already enabled him to produce the seven or eight books which were likely to be the main body of his life's work. He would never have dared to become a householder, and thus receive his rents, without Brownie. He would never have managed to write as much, and thus realise some of his ambitions, without Brownie. He followed his vocation, or prosecuted his trade, resolutely. No doubt in different circumstances, say in that garret in the suburbs, in between grubbing round for a living wage, he would have tried to scribble. But he was not cut out for competition against the odds in an exhausting distracting worldly obstacle race. To write well and do a nine-to-five job is to refute history. He was too modest to aspire to be one of the gallant exceptions that prove that rule. For, with apologies to idealists, literature and art and culture are flowers that grow from the root of all evil : and money is hardly ever earned by artists and writers – or writers who are artists – when they need it. As it was, and had been for fifteen years, he could afford to buy not only his daily bread, but the sustenance equally vital to his spirit – time. He could wallow in the im-material luxury of redundant energy which is the stuff of inspiration. Moreover his privacy was guarded and his routine doubly regulated, his loneliness alleviated, his blacker moods lightened, his necessary obsessiveness laughed into proportion and his very health maintained – by Brownie.

'They say that no man is a hero to his valet,' he observed. 'But my valet's a hero to me.'

There was a touch of Pygmalion in Hereward's attitude. His gratitude and admiration were tinged with pride. Brownie who had conquered an addiction supposed to be almost un-conquerable, who seemed to have emerged unscathed and unscarred from the struggle, who was the embodiment of a success story – and had helped him to succeed – was in a sense his creation as well as his creature.

He claimed that he learned more from Brownie than he had ever taught.

Once he referred to a bereaved widower of his acquaintance, who had been happily married for half a century.

'He talked about his wife. He was in tears. He's turned against the house where they lived together. His children are kind, but busy. I felt so sorry for him.'

'Well, I don't,' Brownie declared. 'He was happy with his old woman for fifty years? And he's got kind children and a house? He's got the lot. He's had his lot. He ought to quit belly-aching.'

No doubt Hereward's exposure to the gritty realism of the representatives of a class lower than his own widened his horizons.

'You Watkinses think you're on the bread-line when we Browns would think we were on the pig's back ... The members of your family kiss each other on the cheek. If we kiss anybody we kiss on the kisser, as if we meant it ... Your ladies wear black clothes – ours never wear black – they wouldn't want to make things any gloomier than they are ... You cry over what we laugh at – if we started crying, where would we stop?'

Brownie was pleased to browbeat his boss with the stick of class-consciousness. But he also personified a summing-up of the pathetic fallacy of egalitarianism and the cause of workers' solidarity. Unlike those at the top of the social pile, who will always unite to defend their advantageous stations in life, he had no reason to defend his native station, he had no feelings of loyalty for his former equals – he despised and was quite ready to betray them in order to overcome his disadvantages.

He considered that he was fundamentally the superior of any man on earth. A certain self-reliant arrogance in him may have been typical of his class. He was chauvinistically vain : he would insist that the British or rather the Scots had won the war, not the Russians and Americans. At the same time he completely dissociated himself from the British post-war worker, for whom he had nothing but scorn.

'He's a lazy skiver on the fiddle – and he lets Commies push him around.'

He was without sympathy for the unemployed.

'They ask for it. They're too greedy for money. They open their mouths too wide – they're not worth the wages they want – of course they lose their jobs. They're *idiotick*!' He pronounced the last syllable of the word with a funny click. 'They hang out their paws for the dole and moan that they can't find employment. But they're stuck-up. Most of them wouldn't work on the buses or sweep the streets, like the blacks. They wouldn't work all hours in a corner-shop and be polite to everybody, like Indians and Pakistanis. Why don't they clean windows ? Why don't they join the army or the police or emigrate ? Why don't they go into private service ?'

He would say less controversially : 'I've been in service on and off for forty years. I couldn't have asked for anything better. I've lived on the fat of the land and never had to pay a penny for it. I've got to know the nobs – it's been interesting.'

And again : 'It's our anniversary, sir. Sixteen years ago today we moved into number 32. Doesn't seem so long, does it ? You've been good to me, I will admit that. I don't believe we've had a single quarrel.'

They would refer with renewed thanks to the ways in which each had rescued the other.

They were indeed the best of friends.

But Brownie had slipped into the habit of addressing Hereward as Master. Perhaps it was meant to be a mark of his respect. It was a joke, too, with a hint of satire. Hereward did not voice any protest, although it worried him slightly. Brownie's five hundred thousand brain-cells were full of paradoxes, if not beeswax. He might have decided to soft-soap his friendly boss or bossy friend by calling him Master, because he had reached the stage of presuming that he was actually in charge.

*

From another point of view the sixteen fruitful years of their association, or twenty-six including the ten at Windle Road, also alarmed Hereward. They were growing older. Brownie might die, which would be bad enough, or retire, which would be worse, or fall ill, which would be worse still – selfishly speaking. He merited a pension if and when he retired : how was it to be paid? Trafalgar Terrace would have to be sold and a proportion of the proceeds converted into some sort of annuity. At a stroke Hereward would therefore lose his servant and friend, his home, his income from lodgers and with it his financial independence and freedom to write.

'I hope you're putting money aside against a rainy day.'

'I've got my nest-egg in the Building Society, Master.'

'You'll need it. I'm afraid I've been very remiss; I've made no provision for your pension. I haven't had the cash – but that's a rotten excuse. Naturally I'll see you're as all right as possible by hook or by crook. But you must save now for your retirement.'

'I'm not retiring.'

'You may one day.'

'I'd go mad if I retired. Work's my everything. I'd be a dead duck without it – or a mad duck.'

'You may change your mind.'

'I won't. I'll die in harness. I'd rather – believe me. That's definite.'

Hereward approached the subject from a different angle.

'Listen, Brownie – I pay you too little. You know why : I'd pay you more if I could : and I know you do pretty well when you cook for other people. But if you're not booked by your clients, you don't receive the weekly wage you deserve.'

'I'm content, Master.'

'Well, I'm not. It doesn't seem fair. And I've been thinking. You should have at least ten active years ahead of you. Why don't you leave me and work for a real millionaire, or pop across to America and be an English butler there, and make a fortune to carry you through your old age?'

'Not likely! In the first place, I've told you, I'll never be that old – I'll die young from knocking my navel out in your service. In the second I can't abide money – I wouldn't cross the road to pick up a five pound note. No, sir! It's kind of you to be concerned about my future. But religion says – or mine does: eat, drink and be merry.'

'Eat and be merry, Brownie.'

'Pardon me – eat and drink lemonade and be merry. No – honestly – I'd work for you for nothing – or just a dry bed to curl up in and a corn of bread.' A corn of bread was his unappetising description of a crust. 'I would, sir! I'm staying put.'

The obstinate implications of Brownie's final declaration worried Hereward yet again.

'What if I went bankrupt and had to sell this house?'

'You won't. And we'd always get by somehow. Besides,

Trafalgar Terrace suits me. I wouldn't want to be anywhere else.'

'But what would you do if I sold it?'

'I'd get a room in the caves.' The caves of the terrace were some slummy boarding-houses along at the far end. 'The shop-keepers are mates of mine: they're always after me to work for them. Or I might look for a job in a wet-fish shop. Nobody likes to work with fish, but I'd love it. And there's a bomb of money in fish.'

'What if I married, Brownie?'

'I'd divorce you, Master. I couldn't stand a woman over me, if you catch my meaning. I'd do my disappearing act – and pronto!'

Hereward was neither bankrupt, nor had he any matrimonial plans, for the time being.

He was touched by Brownie's offer to remain at his post for no pay whatsoever.

But his anxieties were far from removed. He could never let Brownie stay put and work for nothing – apart from the objective rights and wrongs of such a course, it would aggravate the sense of obligation he was already labouring under. And supposing Brownie were to take refuge in the caves for one reason or another, Hereward's inescapable duty would nonetheless be to prove his gratitude in financial terms and at exorbitant cost.

It occurred to him that he had tied their destinies in a knot which, if ever loosed, would unravel the whole fabric of his life.

Sometimes Brownie picked at the sore point in his boss's conscience. He would produce advertisements for qualified menservants culled from newspapers.

'Look at this one, Master: self-contained flat, car, five-day week, eight-hour working day, colour TV, foreign travel, and wages that are plain ridiculous.'

Maybe he was merely drawing attention to his disinterested loyalty.

But he made Hereward wince.

'Why don't you apply for the job?'

'No, thanks! It smells to me. In return for all that cash, whatever would a gentleman be wanting a servant to do for him?'

'Take a chance – you're not exactly innocent – pocket the wages even if they are the wages of sin – follow the advice I've been giving you!'

'Sir! My birthsign's Virgo, sir! I'm the only virgin in Trafalgar Terrace. I'd rather be poor and keep my virtue in one piece.'

Before the prospect of Brownie falling ill and becoming an invalid and a millstone, Hereward simply quailed: and illness was Brownie's main defence against his mortal enemy – boredom.

To amuse himself, or torment his boss in his intuitive teasing way, or both, he would invent lists of terrifying symptoms: difficulty with his speech, paralysis of an extremity, shooting internal pains, partial blindness, unbearably severe headaches. He was such an extraordinary actor that he could assume at will a facial expression of suffering bravely borne, or contort his hands into rheumatoid shapes. He enjoyed every minute of the rigmarole of playing the sick hero: yielding unwillingly to persuasion to seek help from the medical profession; bidding everybody farewell as he sallied forth to surgery or casualty department; comforting his fellow-patients with his devil-may-care jokes; swapping scabrous witticisms with buxom nurses; deceiving doctors; waltzing home with his bouquet of compliments – 'I never thought I'd have a good laugh in the waiting-room, Mr Brown! You're a tough egg and no mistake, Mr Brown!' – and then snapping his fingers at science and at fate by swallowing his supply of pills in a single gulp.

As a rule his own GP, a German refugee named Mannrich, pronounced *Mannrick* with a click by Brownie, called his bluff.

A poisoned whitlow under a fingernail was at last submitted to Dr Mannrich's examination.

'I can get rid of that for you.'

'Thank you, Doctor.'

'I can get rid of it quickly or slowly – which would you prefer, Mr Brown?'

'Quickly, Doctor, please – you don't know my boss – he's pitiless – he won't let me off work for half a day.'

'So – I can get rid of it quickly – but can you stand pain?'

'Doctor, I was in the Black Watch!'

Whereupon the whitlow was gouged out with a scalpel.

'Could you stand it, Brownie?'

'No, Master – I hollered!'

Dr Mannrich summarily dismissed the majority of Brownie's ailments. And Hereward did likewise. But once Hereward mistook what must have been a bout of pneumonia for a bad cold; he was full of rallying exhortations and references to Sir Laurence Olivier when he should have sympathised and served tea etcetera in his turn; and he was not allowed to forget it. He had to be more careful thereafter.

Moreover he and no doubt Dr Mannrich were cognisant of the threat of the card up Brownie's sleeve: their memories were jogged.

'What is it this time?'

'Nothing, sir – just my knee.'

'Do you mean your housemaid's knee? Or should I say your war-wound?'

'Have a heart, sir. I couldn't sleep with it last night. And my head's pounding like Big Ben, although I've munched a packet of Aspirin.'

'Oh well, what can you expect? Your cures are much worse for you than your diseases.'

'I had the headache first, sir. That's why I munched the Aspirin. I was never one to complain – '

'What are you doing now?'

'Explaining, not complaining, sir. I don't mind being ill. But headaches are something else. They put me in mind of my mother.'

'Whereabouts in your head is this headache of yours?'

'Behind my right eye.'

'But it couldn't be a tumour, Brownie. You haven't developed any new tumours for years.'

'Oh yes, sir, I have. The other day a couple came up on my big toe. Would you like to see?'

'No, thanks! How long have you had your headache?'

'A fortnight.'

'You never mentioned it.'

'I didn't want you to fret, sir.'

'Tell me another!'

'I'm telling you the truth, Master. May I go blind and bonkers and die in agony if I'm not!'

'In that case you'd better hurry along to your doctor.'

The word doctor was apt to promote a magical improvement in Brownie's condition. Yet he carried his pantomimes so far that he could not always wriggle out of their consequences. He was compelled to totter to the surgery of Dr Mannrich, who, again, had no alternative except to send the probably hypochondriacal but possibly moribund patient to a hospital for still more tests.

Brownie would return to Trafalgar Terrace beaming.

'How did you get on?'

'I had loads of fun, Master. The nurse who looked after me was a little blood-orange.'

'What about your headache?'

'They passed me A1.'

'Well – thank God.'

*

At such moments Hereward's relief was greater than his annoyance with Brownie for crying wolf. The homily he had prepared on the subject of blackmail boiled down to a glad speechless smile. For if Brownie had been as ill as he pretended, and had not died but had become more or less incapacitated, he would have been the complete financial and even the physical responsibility of his master and friend. Hereward's recurrent nightmare was that he would never be able to free himself from the debt owing to his stricken invalid of a servant, who might refuse to leave his house, who might have to be served and tended for ever. He could hardly scold Brownie for providing evidence that his nightmare was only a dream. He felt more than relieved. He was reprieved – temporarily.

In fact Brownie's constitution was strong but delicate. It was like his physique. He was indeed built on the lines of a bison, or a heavyweight wrestler: his powerful muscles were concealed by layers of protective flesh. At the same time he was the opposite of clumsy and could mend watches with his short thick fingers. His reserves of energy were almost inexhaustible and he seldom spent a day in bed. On the other hand he usually and genuinely had something the matter with him, a graveyard cough, a digestive disorder, a sprain or rheumatics or toothache.

Equally his nervous system, given a chance, was strong. He would not have tempted providence with his dire hints of tumours if he had been – say – as highly-strung as Hereward, and apprehensive and superstitious. He would neither have deliberately got into nor been able coolly to get out of his various scrapes. An element of his nature was imperturbability: he could not have cooked so well without it. Yet he was sensitive, easily upset by lack of appreciation and hostile criticism, excitable to a fault, and, while never moody, prone to panic and despair, for instance at the time of his divorce.

Of course he was drinking then. Drink had reduced him to a nervous wreck. There had been no signs of his being sucked back into or towards the vortex of addiction during his decade and a half at Trafalgar Terrace. Once or twice in the early days he smelt of beer, and he talked too much and his speech seemed to be slurred. But, as he put it, his boss had jumped on him. The intervals between these unpleasant episodes lengthened. Sobriety became the rule of the house rather than the exception.

Hereward's confidence in Brownie and Brownie's confidence in himself advanced in unison. They often discussed drink, congratulating each other on their emergence from the crisis it had caused.

'I do admire you for kicking the habit, Brownie – I don't know how you pulled it off.'

'I couldn't if you hadn't stood by me, Master. You've been a brick' – and so on.

They dwelt sanguinely on their precautions against a repeat performance of the dramas of Windle Road: the bareness of Hereward's drink cupboard, and his determination to check the slightest excess on the part of his version of Galatea; and Brownie's claim that he was allergic to alcohol since his treatment in hospital for schizophrenia or whatever, and his resistance to social life and its temptations, and his healthy dread of pubs. He no longer spent his annual holidays at Butlin's Camps with their bars – he went to his daughter who could be relied upon to keep him out of them. And he stayed with his brother Arthur, surely a model citizen, a skilled engineer by trade, now retired.

If Hereward was going to Watkins Hall for the weekend, he would urge Brownie to visit Arthur. For all his confidence he did not quite like to leave Brownie alone at Trafalgar Terrace.

But the passage of every temperate year helped to dispel his doubts. He was able to return home without a pessimistic sinking of his heart, even if Brownie had been on his own for a whole week or more. Slowly and after many tests and much reinforcement, trust was built up.

Unnecessary, unacceptable as the thought might be, that trust could only be demolished in the same way.

Sometimes Brownie saw his sister Ada and brother-in-law Jack, who was a thriving builder in the north of England: Ada was one of the two sisters whose bed he had shared when he was a boy.

She wrote him exclamatory letters in a sort of transatlantic jargon to arrange meetings during Jack's business trips to London: 'Hi, lover-boy! How's tricks? We're rolling down the great white highway next Tuesday forenoon! Let's hit the town together! Mosey along to our usual dive at opening time! Bye, toots! Ever your kissable . . .'

After an evening with Ada and Jack, Brownie would enumerate the drinks he had had in a defiant tone of voice:

two lagers with lime, a third of a bottle of hock, and a nightcap of another lager.

'But I don't mind you drinking so long as you're in control of the drink and not controlled by it.'

'I've got it under my thumb.'

'Well, that's okay. Did you enjoy yourself?'

'Yes, thank you, Master. It was a riot. I sent for the head waiter in the restaurant and pulled his ears about the temperature of the wine. Ada wet herself. And we were dancing in Piccadilly Circus at two o'clock in the morning.'

The even tenor life at Trafalgar Terrace was resumed. Brownie did not appear to be unsettled by the odd celebration, while Hereward reflected that a change was probably good for him. The contradiction between his allergy to alcohol and enjoyment of lager and hock was somehow glossed over.

He continued to affect an absolute horror of all things alcoholic. If he was asked to sniff the dregs of a bottle of sherry which might have turned sour, he would warn that he was liable to vomit and beg to be excused. If he washed up empty beer glasses – and Hereward was present in the kitchen – he would hold them at arm's-length, averting his head and wrinkling his nose. Should wine be required for an unexpected guest at the last minute, he would protest at having to enter the adjacent pub in order to buy it.

On summer afternoons idle men with newspapers under their arms hung around outside the betting-shop or sat on the walls of front gardens in the terrace.

'Who are those men? What are they doing?'

'They're waiting for the pub to open. They're alcoholics, sir.'

Brownie was disapproving.

'Haven't they got jobs?'

'Some have. That one in the cloth cap – he runs a painting and decorating business from the saloon bar. But most of them are fit for nothing – or they're villains. The fellow with the brief-case deals in jewellery. He drinks neat gin. He's a terrible alkie.'

On another occasion Brownie remarked darkly: 'Burglars use our pub. I'm telling you, sir! That's why we don't get burgled.'

Again the contradiction between his showy reluctance to cross the pub's threshold for wine for his boss, and his intimate knowledge of who drank there and what they drank, was not explained. Brownie, if pressed, probably would have said that he had been gossiping with his friend the landlord. But how had they become friendly? When and where did he gossip with the landlord, who was hard at work every day? And what was his link with the thirsty burglars for whom number 32 was out of bounds?

Alcohol in the abstract, as a conversational topic, had clearly never lost its fascination for him. He would describe in exhaustive detail the merits and demerits of different beers and spirits. He derived a competitive satisfaction from being able to teach Hereward a trick or two.

'We ought to go on a pub-crawl together, Master. It'd make a break – just once! We'd start with a couple of pints apiece of best bitter from the wood at the old *Flying Cow* in Shepherd Market. Then we'd quick-march over the road to the *Shillelagh* in Half Moon Street to lubricate our tonsils with draught Guinness. Then we'd whip in to the *Tartan Banner* in Dover Street for a few drams of the water of life – a backyard brew from the Highlands that curls your hair. Then we'd snatch a fish supper and some noggins of light ale at the *Winkle and Shell* in Soho. And we'd finish with hot toddies at the *Dirk and Sporran* in Shaftesbury Avenue. And I'd carry you home.'

'You'd have to carry me home long before we got to the *Dirk and Sporran*. I can only drink half a pint of beer at a time.'

'Not with me you wouldn't! I wouldn't be seen dead with a half-pint man. Queers drink half-pints.'

Considering Brownie had avoided pubs like the plague for at least sixteen years – or so he said – his memory for their names was remarkable.

For that matter, considering he rarely went anywhere except to the residences of his clients, and of his daughter and brother, and exclusively patronised local shops, how was it that he had such a wide circle of acquaintance?

As well as embarrassing his boss, he could be embarrassed, for instance on expeditions to distant parts of the metropolis. A red-nosed codger with bleary eyes or a peroxided gap-toothed baggage with a ginny voice would fall on his neck at an underground station or a bus-stop.

'Brownie! Billy! Kitch! Terry! My old cock-sparrow! Where have you been shunted? What have you been at? Now don't you run away!'

But he did run, blushing. He was unresponsive and offhand.

'Who was he? Who was she, Brownie?'

'Oh – mates from years back.'

'How many years back? They recognised you without any difficulty.'

'I must be well preserved.'

'And why did they call you Terry? Terry sounds like an alias to me.'

'I've been called worse than that. The other day you were surprised I could remember the names of pubs. In some places they call me Jumbo, because I never forget.'

'Well – you seem to know a hell of a lot of people.'
'I know the whole world, Master.'

*

There still appeared to be no need to elicit straight answers to these questions. Brownie was – or was seen by Hereward to be – sober. It was inconceivable that the mutual trust they had built up brick by brick, behind and beneath which they had as it were sheltered from so many storms, could collapse like a house of cards.

Hereward shrank from contemplation of such a disappointment and catastrophe.

But the answer to one question was brought home to him by an external agency. He had wondered why Brownie had been dropped by several of his clients, including Mrs Pemberton-Wicklow. Hereward met her at a social gathering and was told a tale nastily reminiscent of Windle Road: ten guests for dinner – interminable delays – uneatable food – no washing-up done – Brownie snoring with his head on the kitchen table – and eventually having to be woken and turfed out.

Then another client telephoned Hereward: she was sorry, but could no longer employ a cook who swigged from a bottle of vodka in front of her children.

He girded his loins for battle.

'I understand from Mrs Pemberton-Wicklow that your last dinner for her was a drunken orgy.'

'Not drunken, sir. I was ill on that day. And I'd swallowed every pill I could lay hands on. She got me wrong.'

'And I hear you take vodka with you when you do dinner parties.'

136

'Vodka? Who have you been talking to?'

'A little bird. I hear you swig vodka in front of children.'

'Oh – that! That wasn't vodka – it was lemonade! I made believe it was vodka to those sneaky children for a giggle.'

'Well, your giggle and your pills are going to cost you money.'

'I don't want money.'

'But I do, Brownie – I want you to have it. I couldn't employ you for the wages I pay if you weren't earning extra money from other people. Don't you see? I wouldn't have the face! Anyway, if you start drinking again you'll be done for – and so will I!'

'I haven't started drinking. Instead of listening to old wives' tales, you should have faith in me.'

'I have! Or I had. I mean – personally I've no complaints. But now I'm worried about what happens when my back's turned.'

'Nothing, Master. My dinners out are exhausting – you wouldn't be able to guess at how much work I get through, shopping and cooking and laying the table and serving a tip-top meal and clearing and cleaning, not to mention travelling. But nothing else happens. I've never once given myself a booster. You tell me not to start tippling again. I can tell you I will start, if you don't stop racking me unfairly.'

Brownie was more formidable than he had been – he had the force of his sixteen reformed years behind him. In a manner of speaking he had broken his bonds and grown accustomed to freedom, which he was evidently determined to defend. Besides, he may have felt it was not any more the exclusive prerogative of his boss to be masterful.

Some of Hereward's counsellors supported Brownie, who ought to be allowed to do as he pleased at his age, have an occasional drink, live his own life for better or worse.

137

Too soon the drinks would not be occasional, Hereward retorted – and then Brownie would not live, he would die, and cause more widespread destruction in the process.

He was nonetheless influenced or attracted by such advice. He was unused to wasting his time and energy in altercation – and unwilling to. He was caught in a cleft stick after all: his puritanism might be counter-productive. He therefore refrained from delving deeper into the matter. He resolved not to base any future case on mere hearsay and suspicion. He settled for blissful ignorance in the meanwhile.

Peace broke out once more.

Yet now Hereward was alerted willy-nilly to changes that had taken place over a long period and without his noticing. Brownie's standards of cleanliness had slipped. His everyday clothes were less presentable. And piles of his dirty buttonless shirts and socks with holes in them accumulated in his bedroom, from which a pungent odour spread through the house.

'Go to the launderette for God's sake, Brownie – you're stinking us out!'

'I am going, Master. I've been trying to go for a fortnight. But you wouldn't let me – you put too much on my plate.'

After an overdue visit to the launderette he would omit to iron the damp washing in plastic bags behind his kitchen chair.

'What's the smell in here?'

'It must be the stew you had for lunch.'

'No – I wouldn't eat anything that smelt so bad – it comes from where you're sitting.'

'Thank you, Master.'

'What's in those bags?'

'My laundry.'

'Haven't you ironed it yet?'

'I haven't had a chance. You're a twenty-four hour job, you are! Anyhow, I've got to wet it and run it through the spin-dryer again.'

'Well, please do. I won't have our kitchen smelling like a rabbit hutch.'

Brownie's aversion to bathing became more marked. Hereward had always had to suggest he should jump into a bath. The main effect was grammatical.

'When did you last have a jump-in?'

Thus a verb became a noun with a new meaning.

'I can't remember.'

'You need one.'

'I don't want my body-oils disappearing down the drain. They're precious, you know – they're pure essence of Brown! And the body-oils of we Romanys keep us sweet.'

'That's where you're wrong.'

He would laugh, and promise to jump in later on, and predictably forget, and still give off his pervasive odour.

'How long have you been wearing your socks?'

Brownie glanced at his wrist-watch.

'Two hours and twenty-three minutes, sir!'

'My nose tells me you were wearing them yesterday and the day before.'

'If you'll forgive my saying so, you're too nosey – that's your trouble, Master. My socks are changed twice daily. My socks aren't to blame – it's my feet. I suffer from an uncommon affliction in the foot department.'

'I bet.'

'Truly, Master. It's the waiter's disease, called Carpet Feet – it comes from walking on carpets and it makes your feet all spongey and sweaty. Everybody on the staff of the Piccadilly Club had it.'

139

'I pity the members.'

'You would be on the side of the members, sir. What about us?'

He was humorous and good-humoured, but less malleable than formerly. He developed an effective contrary method of dealing with Hereward's corrections. His revenge for remarks critical of the smelliness of his bedroom and kitchen was to open the windows and doors wide even in winter.

'The house is freezing.'

'I'm airing my room, Master. I'd hate to have a frowsty room like yours. I keep my room fresh.'

'Well, I'm damn cold.'

'Are you, sir? You must be sickening for 'flu. I think it's healthy.'

Following weekend visits to his daughter or brother, when Hereward pointed to the unwashed crockery regimentally stacked in a kitchen cupboard, he would say: 'I'll see to it, sir. But what do you expect? You shouldn't have ordered me to cook your lunch on Saturday morning, and get your shopping, and press your suits, and have my jump-in and thoroughly scrub my feet, as well as cleaning the whole house. My mother wasn't frightened by an octopus – I've only the one pair of hands.'

Hereward was penalised for his slightest requests for service over and above Brownie's idea of duty. For instance, if he asked for the replenishment of a salt-cellar, it would be filled so full of salt that some was bound to be spilled.

'Look at this mess, sir!'

'Sorry, Brownie – but you filled the thing too full.'

'Of course it's my fault. Who wanted me to fill it? Well – it's your table.'

'All right – I'll sweep the salt off the table.'

'You wouldn't know how! Leave it to Brownie! Why keep a dog and bark yourself?'

*

He was more long-suffering, more the martyr, and his retaliatory teasing had a sharper edge.

If Hereward mentioned a dripping tap, Brownie would screw it so tight that nobody else could unscrew it. If Hereward said his bacon was over-cooked, Brownie would serve nearly raw bacon the next time round.

And the slanderous stories he spread grew taller.

A simple-minded neighbour enquired of Hereward: 'It's not true, is it, that you put on a special black top-hat before you sit down to dinner?'

Another neighbour remarked: 'You're a wonder, Mr Watkins – eating so much and keeping so thin! I'm sure that if I ate four meat meals a day I'd burst.'

Once a strait-laced spinster of advanced years buttonholed Hereward in the street: 'Can I speak to you for a moment, Mr Watkins? I received a postcard this morning. It was from the sea-side – one of those sea-side postcards – it really shocked me. I've heard that your Mr Brown is on holiday. And I can't be certain, because nothing was written on the postcard except my name and address, but I think he must have sent it. Will you please tell him I was not amused? I've had palpitations ever since I set eyes on the disgusting object!'

The excessive side of Brownie's nature was definitely gaining ground. A lady-client of his rang Hereward to say she could never again employ such a talkative butler: the previous evening neither she nor her guests had been able to get a word in. And Hereward had to agree that he saw her point. Now and then he was asked by his friends to parties at which Brownie officiated. The food and the way it was served might be miraculous. On the other hand, if Brownie was elated or flustered, the proceedings were in danger of deteriorating into farce. He dominated every conversation; his *soufflés* subsided, or his *pommes fantastiques* were so crisp that they broke somebody's tooth; he would electrify respectable members of the fair sex with his flirtatious compliments and endearments – 'It's your low-cut dress that's making my platter wobble, dearest Madame!'; or he would puff and blow and sweat and curse and speak disrespectfully to dignified gentlemen – 'Mind your back, dear sir! And don't you dare drop the serving spoon into my o-h-range sauce!'

One evening Hereward arrived at a cocktail party at which Brownie, instead of dispensing refreshments, was swaying on his feet and holding forth, announcing to all and sundry that he had been the *chef de cuisine* of General de Gaulle.

Hereward deduced he was drunk and said as much. Brownie denied the charge and stalked off angrily. Ten minutes later he reappeared stone cold sober.

How was it possible? What had happened?

Smart social occasions were apt to go to his head. A snobbish manic mood must have created a false impression of drunkenness. But underlying Hereward's immediate relief was his unease, which was becoming chronic. The mysteries he was afraid to plumb were multiplying, almost as they had in the old days.

In the kitchen at Trafalgar Terrace a photograph was added to the display on Brownie's shelves. It was of a young girl in silhouette on the seashore, posing prettily and provocatively in clinging jeans and jersey.

'Where did you get the pin-up?'

'Ask no questions and you'll be told no lies.'

'Come on, Brownie – if you didn't want me to ask about it you wouldn't have put it there – who is she?'

'She's a nymphomaniac and dipsomaniac and drug-addict.'

'Do you know her well?'

'I know her a bit.'

'I suppose you know the nymphomaniac bit of her?'

'Please, sir – she's just a child – she could be my daughter.'

'Female children are in trouble when you're on their trail. What's she called?'

'Brett.'

'That's an odd name.'

'It suits her.'

'Where does she live?'

'In a flat across the road.'

'Is she married?'

'No, sir.'

'Who pays for the flat? What does she do for a living?'

'She's sitting on a fortune – and not always sitting on it either.'

'Do you mean she's a prostitute?'

'She needs the money to buy her drink and drugs.'

'What sort of drugs?'

'All sorts.'

'She sounds a caution.'

'She is, sir – but lovely with it.'

Hereward did not take much notice. Brownie had been keen on innumerable stray girls before. But he seemed to be particularly intrigued by the cautionary aspect of Brett.

'She'll go with any buck nigger with half a barrel of beer inside him and a fiver in his pocket. I've told her she'll get her throat slit one of these days or nights. But she only laughs at me . . . She's over the top most of the time – she's no idea where she is – on her head or her heels or her back . . . She was a photographic model. She's got a little figure on her fit to make your mouth water. But she couldn't do a job of work any more. It's stupid really . . .'

He sympathised with Brett's stupidity for personal reasons.

'She's got everything – everything's in the right place – and there couldn't be no one nicer when she's talking sense – you'd agree with me, Master! But she's hitting it too hard. She'll be pushing up the daisies before she's thirty.'

'You're sorry for her, aren't you?'

'I can't help it. She reminds me of how I used to be. Do you remember, Master?'

'Do I not!'

'I keep on telling her about the patients in my hospital. I'd like to stop her zonking herself out of her mind with those blasted drugs at any rate.'

'What age is she?'

'Twenty-two – and life is so sweet.'

Hereward was more impressed. He grasped the fact that Brownie's feelings for Brett differed from other passing fancies. Apparently she had tapped the rich seam of his capacity for looking after people. In that case, if he was attempting to cure her of her addiction, he was the less likely to set a bad example by capitulating to his own.

Perhaps Hereward's wishful thinking was partly due to his being on the point of publishing his engagement to be married.

144

6

Brownie was the first person to whom he broke the news.

He had dreaded having to do it. He appreciated that his marriage was going to be a body-blow to his so-called servant – the sweetness of whose life for getting on for thirty years was attributable to the bachelorhood of his so-called master. He foresaw stormy weather, trials and tribulations for both of them, and indeed for Alice.

Brownie's spontaneous response was altruistically joyful. It revealed anew the excellence of his character and the largeness of his heart.

Hereward was at once reassured and almost sad to be happy at his expense. But he had never and could not have taken a vow of permanent celibacy for the sake of Brownie's peace of mind. From the beginning the mutual risk of matrimony had been an integral term of the contract they had entered into.

By accident or by design Hereward had recently arrived at his more optimistic estimate of Brownie's chances of survival. He would have married his Alice whatever the physical and moral state of any outsider. At the same time he was or chose to be encouraged by Brownie's attitude to Brett : which seemed to suggest his dependent and responsibility was at last so independent and responsible that he could look after another person in peril as well as himself.

Nevertheless Hereward wound up their conversation by saying: 'You won't worry, will you, Brownie? I don't know exactly what's in store – it's early days yet. You asked me once to have faith in you. Please have faith in me. But I can promise you here and now that I'll make sure your future's better than your past, provided you don't rush me.'

'I'll be all right, Master. It's you that mustn't worry.'

The two essential questions, whether or not Hereward and Alice would require his services, and whether or not Brownie would do his disappearing act as planned, were left hanging in the air.

In the circumstances they had to be. Hereward was preoccupied for – and by – the present. He was in his late forties: he was not in a position to procrastinate. He had met Alice in the autumn, their wedding was in January, and they set off for their honeymoon, having taken more than enough important decisions.

As for Brownie, he was over sixty. Where would or could he disappear to? He was too old to slink into the caves of Trafalgar Terrace and work in a wet-fish shop. He was too young and active to retire. Naturally he wanted to wait and see.

The period of general uncertainty was not necessarily more of a strain for Brownie than for Hereward, who had already reached private conclusions as daunting as they were inevitable.

Alice was exceptionally kind and good. But she had married one man, not two. Because she did not know Brownie well, she still regarded him as a shabby appendage with a lah-di-dah manner and an inflated reputation for wit: she felt like the singular child in the fable who realised the Emperor had no clothes on. And she was alarmed at the prospect of having to start life with her husband, and cook and care for him, under the eye of a professional who was probably jealous and possessive.

Equally Hereward could not start life with his wife on such an unsteady triangular footing, let alone expose her to the threats he had quailed before: Brownie falling ill and becoming a burden. For he had no doubt she would grow fonder of Brownie – and, if so, that she would be quite incapable of self-protective ruthlessness, in spite of having to bear the brunt of feeding and cherishing the dear invalid.

Hereward quailed worse than ever when he thought of Alice's involvement in that eventuality. And supposing Brownie was driven back to drink by subordination to a woman, what then?

On a less horrific level, Hereward recognised that Brownie's ingrained eccentricities – his bragging and bullshit, his blaring telly, his trailing clouds of tobacco smoke, his unwillingness to jump in, his odoriferous socks, his contrary reactions to correction and presumptions that he was or had been in charge – would never fit into the clean quiet fragrant home of Alice's fancy.

He recalled the apposite proverb and had to agree with it: new wine could not be put in old bottles.

Moreover, while on his honeymoon, he settled with Alice where that home would be: her flat in Pimlico rather than his house in Hampstead. It was more central and convenient, it had rooms of a better size and shape, it was not expensive; and she was attached to it, and for him it was only fraught with pleasant associations. It lacked accommodation for Brownie.

Hereward administered the bitter pill as soon as he dared, coating it liberally with sugar.

'Brownie – I expect you've been wondering what our plans are.'

'Yes, Master.'

'Well – it's no good thinking the three of us will be able to live together happily ever after.'

'No, Master.'

'You're a marvel, but you might get on Alice's nerves if you shared a kitchen. And she's a marvel, yet I know from experience that she'd get on yours.'

'Oh no, she wouldn't.'

'But you always warned me you'd hate to work for any female.'

'Beg pardon, sir – Madame isn't any female.'

'No – of course not – but what I'm trying to say is – we've decided to live in her place. Hang on! Wait a tick! We'll be there – but we're hoping you'll stay on in Trafalgar Terrace. You could come and do for us in the mornings and leave after lunch and attend to the house and the lodgers. What about it?'

'Thank you, sir.'

'Don't thank me. Do you like the idea?'

'I'd like to stay in my bedroom and my kitchen, if possible, sir.'

'I'm telling you that you can. But I'm afraid you won't be so fully occupied as you have been.'

Brownie was provoked to forget that he was being martyrised and ought to act accordingly. He expostulated. He ran through his usual repertoire of proof of his intolerable load of work.

'I'll be more occupied, not less. I'll have another dwelling on my hands, I'll be travelling two or three hours a day – and you'll want extra lodgers in your rooms to help pay expenses. I won't have time to light my pipe!'

'Well – is it going to be too much for you?'

'No! We Browns are not like you Watkinses. We never give in.'

148

'And I don't have to mention the condition, do I?'

'What condition? I might have guessed there'd be a catch in it somewhere.'

'Alcohol's not allowed.'

'Sir, if you asked me open a can of beer, I wouldn't remember how.'

'One more thing, Brownie: do you think you'll be lonely in the evenings without me?'

'I'll be glad to have a bit of rest and relaxation for a change.'

*

It was easier than Hereward had anticipated. Brownie had been fairly receptive and adaptable in principle. Anyway he had ended by laughing at the dislocation of his existence.

Hereward and Alice spent some months at the house in Trafalgar Terrace, while the flat in Suffolk Crescent was converted and decorated for their joint use.

And Brownie dropped his defences against Alice. He talked Cockney in her company, he was comical, coarse, and gentle and tactful. As a result she withdrew her reservations. She was charmed by his talents and sunny willing temper. She was spellbound by his stories of the Piccadilly Club and his military misadventures – and amused when she heard him spouting German to the milkman, who had also been in a prisoner of war camp. She asked him for recipes, which he wrote out wrong in his flowery script. She let him try to blind her with the science of his cookery. She commiserated when he said he had done his stretch of thirty years hard labour for Hereward. She was tolerant of his other peccadillos.

Her more friendly feelings were reciprocated.

Brownie conceded to his boss: 'She's tops – you don't deserve her.'

Then Hereward and Alice returned a day earlier than expected from a visit to relations to discover Brownie inebriated.

His explanation was that he had been to a friend's funeral and later drunk a single toast to the deceased – and the wine must have been either corked or spiked.

In private Alice interceded on his behalf.

'He only had one glass of wine.'

'Don't you believe it!'

'And he had been to a funeral.'

'Funeral my eye!'

'And the wine might have disagreed with him.'

'If he really was at a funeral, the wine wouldn't have been spiked. Nobody spikes the wine at funerals.'

'But you can't stop him doing what he wants to do in his spare time. It's not possible. It's not your business.'

'He wouldn't be here today if I hadn't made it my business.'

'Well, please, for my sake, give him another chance.'

'Give him a quarter of an inch and he'll take a mile.'

'I suppose you know best.'

'I should – I've reason to!'

All the same Alice soothed the savage breast of her spouse, who accepted Brownie's apologies and confined himself to a mild regretful rebuke.

The following morning he found a note slipped under the door of the conjugal bedroom.

It ran: 'Dearest Madame and Master – P.G. Tips from now on – Your Devoted and obedient servant, Brownie.'

Alice's argument in favour of forbearance seemed to be supported by events. Brownie recovered his equilibrium. His behaviour was faultless. Hereward had to admit he was pleased that his dictatorial impulse had been curbed.

Then – again – a week or so before the Watkinses moved into Suffolk Crescent they were invited to a buffet supper which Brownie was to cook for his client and their hostess. They arrived, were admitted by a hirsute Portuguese maid, were greeted and introduced to guests, and saw Brownie staggering round in the supper room, grinning foolishly and with his black bow-tie awry.

Hereward sought him out and hissed at him: 'You're drunk!'

'Oh sir! Hullo, sir! No, sir, not drunk, sir!'

'Yes, you are! How could you? I'm ashamed of you!'

Brownie, instead of meekly bowing his head according to custom, laughed in a recalcitrant jeering way and summoned the maid from the kitchen: 'Angelina! Come and get an earful of how my master speaks to me!'

Hereward commanded: 'Shut up, Brownie! Pull yourself together!'

But Brownie continued to address Angelina: 'Listen to him! That's how he always speaks to me! I told you, didn't I? He's worse than Hitler! He thinks he owns me!'

Hereward was forced to beat a retreat. The evening was ruined for him, even if the disasters he was expecting did not quite materialise – and although in Alice's opinion Brownie got through it amazingly well. The next day the traditional accusations and warnings and excuses and apologies were exchanged.

Yet an alien element had stolen into the routine. Hereward had not only criticised, he had been subjected to offensive criticism for the first time. The episode in the supper room was a sort of joke: in retrospect he saw its funny side. It was also a raising of the standard of revolt, however shakily.

The disturbing implication was that Brownie was tearing up the treaty on which he seemed to consider his master had already defaulted by marrying. He was declaring his intention not to abide by the provisions of it unilaterally, after the other signatory had repudiated them. He had revealed his reproachfulness and resentment, his sense of being the loser in his competition with his boss, his sense of being morally and metaphysically betrayed and abandoned.

His actions hinted at the new-fangled notion that drink was and would be not his downfall, but the remedy for his wounds – and his secret weapon in the next stage of the war he had to fight in self-defence.

Things returned almost to normal. The surface of the relationships at number 32 was once more unruffled. The armistice was brief. Hereward was dismayed by snippets of terrace gossip that reached him. Evidently Brownie was making references to redundancy payments. He was telling people he would take his boss to the cleaners if there was ever any question of unlawful dismissal.

To add to Hereward's anxieties as an employer, Alice's work would necessitate a trip abroad immediately after their removal into Suffolk Crescent – and it was fixed that he should accompany her.

'How long will you be out of the country, Master?'

'Two or three months – I don't know.'

'It'll be a nice holiday.'

'It won't be exactly a holiday. Alice has got her job to see to, and I'll be writing.'

'What am I meant to do?'

'You'll have the house and the lodgers, and our flat to keep an eye on. And I was hoping it'd be a break for you, too.'

'I'll be lucky!'

'But, Brownie, you must agree you'll be less busy than if you had the house and lodgers and us to clean and cook for into the bargain! Do you think you'll be able to manage?'

'Oh – I can manage!'

'You won't do anything silly? You'll be here on your own, remember.'

'On my own? I'll have the lodgers badgering me twenty-four hours a day.'

'Well – it's an experiment. Give it a whirl, Brownie! You say they're my lodgers. But they're your bread and butter. If you decide you don't like these new arrangements, we'll put our heads together and devise something different. I promised you, didn't I?'

'Yes, Master.'

'Listen – surely I've proved that you needn't feel insecure? I'm determined to get you suited, if it kills me.'

'I'm not complaining.'

'Not much.'

'Why – what have I said? I never complain. I may moan, but I don't complain. No! I'll be fine – I'll be having a high old time – that's fair, isn't it? You've got Madame – you worry about her! And you ought to follow my advice: just live for each other and let the world take care of itself.'

*

Hereward did so for three months.

But back in England, installed with Alice in Suffolk Crescent, he was informed by Brownie that their world had not taken care of itself after all.

Everything was wrong.

The lodgers had been playing up, not paying rent, subletting their rooms, harbouring undesirable personages, causing disturbances, and disobeying and abusing Brownie.

'You're too kind to them.'

'I knew it'd be my fault.'

'But you are too kind.'

'I was too kind to say I'd be responsible for that lot of pigs' blurts!'

One lodger had done a moonlit flit, owing both Brownie and Hereward a packet of money, and in due course compelling his landlord to sue for the forfeiture of his lease.

'Did you lend him money, Brownie?'

'No – but I kept an account for him.'

'In other words you did lend him money. I suppose you did his shopping?'

'Well – he was always asking me out to dinner.'

'Did you go?'

'Once or twice.'

'Where?'

'To the Wine and Cheese Bar.'

'What did you drink with your cheese?'

'Have a guess! I'd fool around with a glass of wine. But he was half an alcoholic. He'd bottle it and then he'd call me a lackey.'

'Have you any idea where he's flitted to?'

'If I had, he'd be singing soprano!'

Alice asked after Brownie's health.

He was not fit. He had never got over his accident: which accident was perhaps too unlikely to be untrue. He had been travelling from Trafalgar Terrace to Suffolk Crescent – he emphasised the point that he was about his boss's business. He was on the escalator in the Underground, when a boy ten yards ahead of him dropped a bundle of cricket stumps. The stumps hit him, tangled with his legs, tripped him, and he twisted and sprained his knee.

'I was black and blue and purple and yellow, Madame, like one of those baboons – except in another place. And my knee's still puffy – and it had to be my dicky knee, didn't it?'

No, far from being fit, he was lame, and his nerves were shot to pieces by the lodgers, and he had this bad arthritis in his hands which made them tremble, and his eyesight was not what it had been.

'Master says the flat's dirty and dusty. But I can't polish for the pain in my hands, Madame. And I can't see a speck of dust.'

He was at loggerheads with members of his family. His brother Arthur had married a year before Hereward, and even later in life. Needless to say Arthur's wife Edith had fallen in love with Brownie.

'She won't leave me be. She's on top of me the moment Arthur turns his head the other way. It's embarrassing, sir!'

Edith must have had a dominant personality. She dressed her conventional old husband in flowered shirts and persuaded him to wear a piece of false hair. At a family function a relative failed to recognise him.

'Who's that over there?'

'That's Arthur,' Brownie replied.

'Arthur? Never! What's he got on his head?'

'He's got a dead cat on his head!'

Marriage had been too much for Arthur, who had recently suffered a stroke and was laid up in hospital. Edith seized her opportunity or tried to: she pestered her brother-in-law to come and visit the sick man. When Brownie rejected these hypocritical appeals, her long telephone calls and letters grew spiteful.

Unfortunately Brownie answered her letters. Although so peaceable in his speech, he was a fire-eater of a correspondent. Edith was infuriated by the scornful home truths in his missives. She dipped her pen in poison in response, and began to ring in the middle of the night in order to wake him and whisper not-so-sweet nothings in his ear.

Apart from his persecution by Edith, which rendered it impossible for him to risk seeing Arthur, he had somehow quarrelled with Ada, with whom he was engaged in another acrimonious correspondence.

Hereward prayed that history was not repeating itself. For nearly two decades he had seemed to be right to deny that portentous dictum. Yet the history in question had been made in a preceding period, when Brownie was similarly troubled by aspects of his occupation, his plethora of ailments, by having the opposite sex at his throat and a stricken brother in the background, and by tremulous hands.

However, Suffolk Crescent received its cleansing blitz in the fullness of time. He arrived there on the dot of eight o'clock every weekday morning. He produced and helped to consume a delicious lunch, as he would and could not have done if he had been drinking deeply – and departed at two or three in the afternoon.

Sometimes in the evenings, should Hereward telephone through to Trafalgar Terrace, he sounded stupefied. But his reasonable excuse was that he had been asleep : because his nights were often disturbed by Edith's irate mating-calls, he was more than ever inclined to drowse in front of the telly.

'And you know me, Master – you could chop off my leg without my noticing when I'm drowsy – forty winks for me are like a general anaesthetic – and it takes me half an hour to come round.'

Occasionally Hereward felt impelled to voice the hackneyed query: 'Were you – are you – will you be really okay?'

Brownie's invariable answer: 'Yes, Master,' proved nothing.

Theoretically he ought to have been okay. He was working in Suffolk Cresecent, not particularly hard, for about thirty hours each week. His services for his lodgers at Trafalgar Terrace were meant to be minimal. His weekends were his own, he was no longer badly paid, he had no obligatory expenses, and could coin money at his clients' parties if he chose to. His conscientious boss was running a whole large house in Hampstead mainly for his benefit.

In practice he still moaned. His journeys to and from Pimlico by public transport were adding four hours daily to the six during which he sweated blood for Hereward. At Trafalgar Terrace he had to put in at least four more hours a day, making a total of ninety in a week. He was too knackered to do dinners for his clients. At weekends he could not enjoy his freedom, he had to rest his weary limbs – and so on.

'Well – cut your hours of work – arrive at the flat at ten in the mornings – it's entirely up to you!'

Brownie squashed such suggestions. He had set his mind on martyrdom. He preferred to blame Hereward – and punish him by being the bearer of bad news.

'I felt giddy on my crowded bus this morning – I thought I was going to flake out . . . A fellow stepped on my big toe with the tumours in the Underground – he must have weighed sixteen stone – it's been merry hell ever since . . . Sorry to interrupt your writing, Master, but I thought you'd like to know the rain's pouring through the ceiling of your old bedroom in Hampstead . . . There are definitely rats in your basement area, Master – I've seen their visiting cards . . .'

Hereward and Alice took to driving him home whenever possible. One afternoon in Trafalgar Terrace they had emerged from the car and were standing by it, when a girl carrying flagons of wine tripped towards them, calling as if to a pet: 'Kitchy – Kitchy – Kitchy – Kitchy – Kitchy – Kitchener!'

She was young and attractive and jolly.

'Don't forget, you're coming to my party tonight, my little Kitchy-Kitchener!' she cried.

Brownie, who had blushed crimson, addressed her in a warning tone: 'These are my bosses.'

'Oh!' She stared at Hereward boldly and curiously. 'So you're the boss!' She obviously knew more about him than he knew of her. 'Well, well!' She laughed and twiddled her fingers at Brownie – 'See you!' – and passed by with the flagons of wine for her party under her arms.

Alice enquired: 'Is that Brett?'

'Yes, Madame.'

'Isn't she sweet?'

'Oh yes, she's sweet enough. She's naughty but she's nice.' Brownie was regaining his composure.

'Is she as naughty as you say? She looks so innocent.'

'That's it, Madame. But innocent's the one thing she never has been. And she's naughty company for me.'

*

The experiment had failed.

After about a year Hereward admitted it. The complicated design for living, which was costing him so dear in time, trouble, money and expense of spirit, had turned into the chief bone of contention between himself and its intended beneficiary. Brownie could cope neither with his novel range of duties nor his extra leisure, he refused to restrict one or the other or both, and was increasingly dissatisfied. He had too much to do, according to the familiar refrain – yet was at a dangerously loose end during his slack evenings and weekends off. If he was not already drowning his sorrows he soon would. Trafalgar Terrace, containing Brett, would then be the reverse of his salvation.

'It hasn't worked out, has it?'

Brownie agreed.

They began to think of alternatives.

The prospects or lack of them depressed Hereward. Whatever scheme he devised Brownie was likely to undermine – later on agreeing with complacence it had not worked out. Even sober and healthy – or fairly – he was threatening to become a millstone. Far from disappearing, he still spoke of dropping dead in harness. He could not be dismissed ungratefully, unlawfully and with an exorbitant golden handshake; he could not be insinuated into the employment of a stranger, who might actually exploit him and would certainly be encouraged to do so; he could not be condemned to solitary confinement in a new house – say a flatlet in the neighbourhood of Suffolk Crescent; and he could not be paid a full wage for part-time service by a boss he had deprived of lodgers and thus of revenue.

His receipt of the old-age pension would be a help.

'How long before you get it, Brownie? How old are you? Let's see – you must be sixty-four.'

Hereward based his calculations on the age of a friend of his, Adam Barlow, of whom Brownie had always made a special fuss, saying they were twins.

'Sixty-four? Don't be funny, Master! I'm coming up to sixty-two.'

'But Mr Barlow's sixty-four – and I thought you were his exact contemporary – you used to say you were and that virgins ought to stick together – have you forgotten?'

'Mr Barlow's birthday and mine fall on the same day – we're both Virgos – but he's my elder by two and a half years if he isn't my better.'

'Believe it or not.'

'I'll fetch you my birth certificate, Master!'

The birth certificate was duly produced. The entry under date of birth corroborated Brownie's claim. But it rather looked to Hereward as if the numerals had been tampered with.

Although the suspicion seemed preposterous, Hereward entertained it sadly. For no doubt Brownie was frightened of being asked to retire – and a spot of forgery would postpone that evil hour. In his present vengeful mood, in order not to mitigate his boss's predicament, he might be prepared to forgo a couple of years of pension.

Yet at last he relented to the extent of contributing an idea of his own to the debate. His client Mrs Hilda Stacey was a well-to-do widow with a house near Suffolk Crescent and accommodation going begging. She had offered him a home and a job at the time of Hereward's marriage.

Could he not live and partly work there?

Hereward wrote to Mrs Stacey, who replied enthusiastically. She was a strong-minded impulsive person, acquainted with and undeterred by Brownie's record. She admired him for having vanquished his vice, she appreciated his virtues, and would like nothing better than to have him in her house. His presence would be protective, and he could occasionally cook for her and her guests in return for a luxurious room and bathroom adjoining her kitchen.

The decision was left to Brownie.

It was explained to him that if he remained at Trafalgar Terrace, unsatisfactory as he found it, he would be safe, whether or not he was ill or got into trouble – at any rate until he reached pensionable age; whereas if Trafalgar Terrace were sold, and Mrs Stacey were to change her mind and evict him for some reason, he would have no roof over his head.

He was warned that Mrs Stacey was not the type to stand for nonsense or nurse him through an illness – and there would be nowhere else for him to go. He himself acknowledged that he was bound to come to grief in a secluded flat. Anyway he and his boss between them could not afford a flat in central London. If their second experiment failed, they would have to part. And even with a subsidy from Hereward in recognition of his services, he – un-pensioned by the state – would be poor. Trafalgar Terrace was still his for the asking – and the dependable and indeed rewarding devil he knew must be preferable.

He settled for Mrs Stacey.

'You're not just being contrary, are you, Brownie? You're not saying yes because I'm half-inclined to think you ought to say no? Are you convinced you couldn't carry on in Hampstead?'

Hereward also enquired: 'Is it that you want to escape from Brett?'

'Brett and others, Master. I need to be shook up. And Mrs Stacey's lovely. And I'll have made it to South West One, where the nobs live. And I'll only have to cross the road to be with you and Madame in Suffolk Crescent.'

Trafalgar Terrace was put on the market. Brownie showed possible purchasers over it. One man who was keen to buy the place mysteriously withdrew his bid. He informed the estate agent he was nervous of another flood.

'What on earth did you tell him, Brownie?'

'Nothing.'

'Did you mention flooding?'

'Well – we were flooded during that freak storm a few years ago.'

'But it was no more than a trickle of water under the basement french window! I suppose you said you could hardly keep your nose above it and were baling out all night?'

He giggled.

But in spite of his salesmanship the house was eventually disposed of.

Meanwhile Hereward had negotiated further with Mrs Stacey and drafted a document, a sort of charter, the prime intention of which was to safeguard Brownie from himself. He was to work for the Watkinses until after lunch for five days a week, and cook for Mrs Stacey and a strictly limited number of her guests on three evenings in lieu of rent. His weekday afternoons, his Tuesday and Thursday evenings, and his Saturdays and Sundays were to be free. The plan would cease to have contractual force in the event of any party to it being unhappy in any way. And Hereward guaranteed to extricate Brownie from Mrs Stacey's ground floor room at short notice, if requested.

Everyone signed on the dotted lines.

7

Trafalgar Terrace was vacated; Brownie moved in with Mrs
Stacey; each was pleased and then delighted with the other;
they could not get over their good luck; and Hereward
wondered if his problem was finally solved.

Life in this context seemed sweet to all, or sweeter. But
the sweetest life cannot be lived without fear of the end of
it, at least.

In the next twelve months Hereward's every fear apper-
taining to Brownie was realised.

Mrs Stacey began to find fault with him. She was sorry
to – she was tentative – she was unused to dealing with menservants – she was appealing to Hereward for advice and
assistance. Brownie was a splendid fellow; but why did he
stack her plates dirty in the kitchen cupboards? Why could
he not buy a shirt that buttoned across his tummy? How
often did he have a bath? Had he always smoked quite so
much of that positively fumigating tobacco? He was too
kind to her, he was spoiling her – for instance he made her
sit down to an elaborate tea although she had never before
bothered with a mid-afternoon meal. Yet the other evening
he had omitted to clear the dining-room table and had not
even extinguished the candles after a party – he had simply
gone to ground; and the lights had blazed in the kitchen and

in his room until dawn, when she heard him washing dishes. It was worrying – candles left burning could cause a fire. Why had he vanished like that?

Soon she herself was able to answer the last of her awkward questions. Right in the middle of a party, between the meat and pudding courses, she had found him either asleep or unconscious in the chair in the kitchen, which reeked of alcohol and looked as if it had been hit by a bomb. She could not rouse him. She had to rescue the remains of the dinner, while he lay there spreadeagled and snoring like a grampus. Later, when she went to bed, he was still in his drunken stupor. It was worse than worrying – it was not nice. A decent woman of her age ought not to have to put up with it. Admittedly she was in receipt of an apologetic note. But how was she to be sure it would not happen again?

Hereward, assured her. Brownie did likewise, having been accused, reproached, racked, implored and reasoned with by his boss. Mrs Stacey was mollified – she now had experience of what a lot she had to lose.

But in private Hereward was as pessimistic about the future as he had ever been optimistic. For Brownie had consigned his copy of the charter to the waste paper basket, practically speaking – and seduced Mrs Stacey into following his example. He not only served her tea when by rights he should have been resting, he fetched her morning paper from the newsagent's in all weathers, he spent his free afternoons shopping for her, and on his evenings off and at weekends he insisted on cooking her three-course snacks. He would not let her into her own kitchen: she reported that she had to choose between being fed by him and starving.

Hereward could imagine it: 'Why keep a dog and bark yourself, Madame? ... Allow me, Madame – I've nothing else

164

to do . . . When I'm not hard at it I feel dead, Madame . . . Who's coming to dinner today?'

Of course Mrs Stacey had never met anyone half as ambiguous. She had not yet learned that when Brownie said one thing he usually meant another. If she expressed a wish to nibble a biscuit and cheese for dinner alone, he seemed so cast down, so sorry for her in her solitude and disappointed for himself, that she rushed to the telephone and mustered an instant party, which he then held against her. She complained of being worn to a frazzle by having to entertain every Tom, Dick and Harry of her acquaintance for the amusement of Brownie, whose complaint was identical. She acceded to his demands for interesting new recipes: he reported that he had to sweat over them for six hours. And her grateful compliments egged him on.

Consequently overwork and exploitation were no longer the theme of his time-honoured radical teasing, but almost a matter of fact. He blamed Mrs Stacey to Hereward, and probably vice versa – while Hereward wrung his hands over the real incorrigible culprit. Under pressure Brownie admitted he had been *idiotick*: but having spoilt Mrs Stacey, how was he suddenly to stop?

He could not mend his characteristic ways. Without exaggeration he was exhausted. And his cure for exhaustion had always been drink.

The only hope was that Hereward and Alice were again going abroad in connection with her job for three months. Certainly Brownie could, and perhaps he would, take it easier during their absence. On the other hand he might cave in completely without his boss to prop him up.

Soon Mrs Stacey was writing the Watkinses desperate letters.

Hereward did not need to read her detailed accounts of the calamities he had dreaded.

On his return he raged at Brownie and sent him straight to the doctor – his hands were palsied and the whites of his eyes bright yellow. And he did his best to convince Mrs Stacey he had not inveigled a total alcoholic into her house by false pretences.

Dr Mannrich tested Brownie's liver and warned that if he went on drinking he would kill himself within a few weeks. As a result there was much talk of P.G. Tips and lemonade henceforth. His health improved. He was given a last chance. His excuses for his collapse in the summer counted for more with Mrs Stacey than with Hereward, who had heard them before: his brother Arthur had one foot in the grave and his virago of a sister-in-law had again got him down, having discovered where he was living. He swore solemn oaths on the heads of his daughter and grandchildren, and so on.

It was too late. Guilt because he had been drinking, or still was, reduced him to being everybody's abject contrite slave. He was the more prodigal of his involuntary and compulsive services for Mrs Stacey. In the mornings, after fetching her newspaper and before he arrived at Suffolk Crescent, he was cooking breakfast for her daily lady, called Noreen. He was doing most of Noreen's household work. He was even shopping for Noreen.

The autumn jolted by.

Christmas came with its festive spirit or spirits.

He was intoxicated for three weeks. Apparently he never went to bed: he slept in Mrs Stacey's kitchen chair at night, snoring and groaning horribly. He slept and groaned in the Watkinses' kitchen by day. He slept if he sat down, and woke drunk if he could be woken. He was incapacitated – and beyond Hereward's authority.

Mrs Stacey invoked the clause of the charter that guaranteed his removal from the wreckage of her ground floor.

Hereward told him.

He added: 'You know it's the end of the road for us.'

*

Brownie was so shocked and startled that he played the trump card he had kept up his sleeve for many years.

He was iller than his master knew. The pain in his head was like a pneumatic drill, he was permanently giddy and dizzy, he had not been able to see properly for ages, and his sleepiness was abnormal. Drink was by no means the whole story.

Hereward packed him off to Dr Mannrich, who fixed an appointment in hospital for the following day.

'He wants them to scan my noddle.'

'But you've had tests in hospital on other occasions.'

'No, Master. It's different this time. Doctor's opinion is that I've started a tumour on the brain.'

'Did he say so?'

'He's afraid so.'

'Truly?'

'Why should I lie to you now?'

Once more Brownie was turning the tables on Hereward.

'When is your appointment?'

'Ten o'clock.'

'Well – please go and rest. And I'll ring you at nine tomorrow.'

'But at eight I'll be trotting round to get breakfast for yourself and Madame.'

'Don't think of it, Brownie! I couldn't bear you to get our breakfast when you're bound to be feeling ropey.'

'I'd rather it was business as usual, Master. I'd rather keep busy while I can.'

'Are you busy this evening? Shall I speak to Mrs Stacey?'

'No, I will.'

'You ought to have an early night.'

'Leave it to me.'

'What? Yes – just as you like. And I'm sorry.'

'Thank you, Master.'

Hereward might have been more sceptical and less sorry, but for Mrs Stacey and Alice.

Mrs Stacey was spoken to – and appalled by her misinterpretation of the issue. Instead of sympathising with and organising prompt medical attention for Brownie, who had heroically striven to do her bidding as he approached the terminal stage of his disease, she had given him two weeks' notice. She had acted heartlessly in her ignorance – thanks to Hereward, she implied. She should have been fully informed about Brownie's tumours, one of which on the brain could account for all his extraordinary behaviour. His drinking was understandable and pardonable – and he was not necessarily fibbing when he said he had never drunk much. Although her unkindness was not her fault, she deeply regretted it.

Alice's regrets were even deeper. Brownie had no home to call his own – and she felt responsible. If she had not spirited Hereward from Trafalgar Terrace, if she had included Brownie in her residential arrangements, he would not have been unsettled, insecure, drunken, harrassed, and perhaps in consequence sick to death. She had grown to love him – and might as well have stuck a knife in his back.

She was aghast at the injustice recently meted out to him. His boss and her husband had been certain he knew better, obviously wrong, and cruel. For he had brushed aside patent symptoms of illness, dismissed pleas of innocence, hounded his faithful retainer to the edge of the abyss, and made a perfect misery of his probable ultimate days.

Hereward's defences crumbled. If the tumour was not a trump card but the lethal reality it was beginning to seem to be, he would never forgive himself. He had judged the present in the light of the evidence from the past – Brownie's alcoholic tendencies, his previous crisis, his play-acting, and inventive genius for extenuating circumstances. Yet the past had been survived: and history was not always repetitive. Error stared him in the face – it would be typical of Brownie to have the last laugh at his expense by dying: in which case his praiseworthy attempt to save Brownie's soul and body, his high-minded hectoring, and rows and recriminations, would look like sheer inexcusable tyranny. His maltreatment of his afflicted benefactor and best friend had already antagonised his wife. He was regarded as a monster by Mrs Stacey – and could be short of time in which to repair the damage he had done.

He dared not argue sceptically. He was sorry for lots of reasons.

He passed a wretched night.

Brownie appeared in the morning. He was punctual and sober. He ate a hearty second breakfast with Hereward and Alice.

'Did you manage to sleep?' Alice asked tearfully.

'Like a top, Madame!'

'You weren't too worried?'

'Worried? No, Madame! I often shook hands with death in the war.'

'Oh, please, Brownie, don't talk like that!'

Hereward broke in: 'You shouldn't have bothered to come

round to be with us. I told you not to. I hoped you'd lie in. Still, it's lovely to catch a glimpse of you.'

'I couldn't have stayed with Mrs Stacey, Master. She saw me off – she got up specially. She was choked!'

'Poor Mrs Stacey!'

'And Noreen was blubbering all over the place.'

'Well, you're everybody's favourite.'

'I know, Master – it's awful!'

Alice asked: 'More tea, Brownie?'

'I wouldn't say no, Madame. Tea's my tipple. I'm like the main drain where tea's concerned.'

He was so brave and cheery, even so challenging with his claim that tea was his tipple, that Hereward felt he could enquire: 'What exactly happened when you went to Dr Mannrich yesterday afternoon?'

'He rang through for today's appointment.'

'At once? Didn't he examine you?'

'He took one look at me and said it.'

'Said what?'

'As I walked into the consulting-room he said: "I can guess why you're here, Mr Brown – it's a tumour on your brain, isn't it?" '

'What an odd thing for a doctor to say!'

'Wasn't it just? It brought me up in goose-pimples. It reminded me of my mother. She died in agony from a brain-tumour, Madame.'

'Yes, I've heard, Brownie.'

'Brownie – would you mind repeating Dr Mannrich's diagnosis? It strikes me as incredibly unprofessional.'

'He looked me straight between the eyes and said: "You've got a tumour on the brain, you have." '

Alice giggled apologetically.

'I wish you wouldn't make it sound funny, Brownie.'

Hereward also laughed a little at the black humour of the situation, and Brownie himself joined in.

'Well – I should be going.'

'Let me drive you to the hospital.'

'Oh no, Master. You get on with your writing – don't let me interrupt it. And I'd prefer to find my own way there.'

'I could keep you company while you were waiting to be X-rayed.'

'For pity's sake, Master – you'd kill me on the spot with embarrassment.' He blushed uncomfortably at the very idea. 'No – I'll telephone as soon as I've any news.'

They said goodbye.

The Watkinses waved at him from a window with their fingers crossed.

He telephoned at mid-day : 'All clear, Master !'

The general relief had its rueful sides.

Hereward was mortified that he at least had not known better than to jump through Brownie's hoops before he needed to. He should have protested that no doctor in his right mind would greet a patient with the words: 'You've got a tumour on the brain, you have.' As likely as not Dr Mannrich's examination had disproved the tumour theory – and the appointment for a brain-scan was another figment of Brownie's dramatic imagination and an unavoidable part of his confidence trick: which would explain his reluctance to be accompanied to the hospital. Naturally, if so, it was easy for him to seem to be brave and to sleep like a top, while the courage of Hereward's sceptical convictions evaporated and he was kept awake by remorse.

The relief was also short-lived.

Doubtless Brownie had made himself feel mortally ill. Conceivably he had hoped that death would spare him dishonour. Whatever occurred or did not occur in that hospital where he might or might not have had an appointment, he must have realised he had run out of excuses and the game was up. He surrendered – to his grief at having got the sack, his humiliation, his horror of retirement, his addiction.

Two or three days later Mrs Stacey, whose anguish had turned into anger, requested Hereward to rid her of the oblivious hulk in her kitchen within twenty-four hours.

*

But the story of William Kitchener Brown was more of a comedy than a tragedy.

Hereward persuaded him that, in accordance with the charter they had signed, he would have to move out of Mrs Stacey's house and into a small hotel nearby, while they worked out the details of his gloomy future.

'At such short notice, Master?'

'Yes, Brownie.'

Again the shock of these rapid developments was sobering. The beeswax cleared from his five hundred thousand brain-cells. He was dignified in defeat, amenable and uncomplaining at last. His valour or lack of it had been a disputatious old joke between himself and Hereward. The argument was settled by his attitude to his latter days stretching ahead, minus his boss, fraught with memories of failure, apparently impoverished, solitary, bleak, and the graveyard of his rare gifts and talents.

Hereward was surprised not only by his stoicism.

When he was helping to pack Brownie's clothes and few belongings – the treasured copies of his own books; the brown-paper-covered cookery books with greasy thumb-marks; the framed photographs and rack of pipes; the collection of ornamental tankards, including that prize for drinking twenty-one pints of beer in an evening – he observed: 'I'd forgotten how many tankards you accumulated over the years.'

'Yes, Master.'

'You bought them in antique shops and curio shops, didn't you?'

'Yes, Master,' he smirked.

'Brownie, were they prizes, too?'

'Yes, Master.'

Hereward ventured further into the maze of his ex-man-servant's secrets.

'When did you start drinking again?'

'Not when you married. You pass the word to Madame She's been an angel to me – I wouldn't want her to think she drove me back to drink. No! I was at it long before. I was sure I could stop the minute I needed to. That was my mistake.'

'Was Brett a bad influence?'

'Yes and no.'

'Who was a bad influence if she wasn't?'

'Arthur.'

'Your brother Arthur – who died a month ago? But I thought he was teetotal! I was always encouraging you to spend your weekends with Arthur! You led me to believe you'd be safe!'

'I know,' Brownie giggled.

He either confessed or seized on the pretext of his late brother, who was in no position to disagree: 'He was worse than me. All my brothers were drunkards. We Browns were born with beer instead of blood in our veins. Edith says I killed Arthur by boozing with him. She's been on and on at me about doing him in. But really it was the other way round.'

Hereward enquired: 'Why didn't you tell me? Why didn't you allow me to help?'

'I was too proud – and craft's my middle name.'

On an unquestionably truthful impulse, when Hereward asked if he would ever cut out alcohol – if he could – if he wished to – he admitted: 'It's my life, Master.'

His fate had been sealed by Mrs Stacey's ultimatum. But his revelations imposed limits on plans for his retirement. It was established that he would live the rest of his life somewhere near his daughter Peggy at Margate in Kent. The Watkinses' initial idea was to settle him in a boarding-house, where he would have the company of his fellow-lodgers and his landlady would fall in love with him. On second thoughts they appreciated that even the most loving landlady might take exception to his anti-social habits, which he had said were unbreakable – especially in the summer season when rooms at a holiday resort were at a premium. He would be better off in a self-contained flat, provided he could afford the rent, was not too lonely, did not let it get too dirty, or annoy his neighbours by singing *Sweet Adeline* and passing out on the staircase. Even a flat purchased for him rather than rented would be subject to the same disadvantages.

For thirty years he had been saying that if he won the football pools he would buy a cottage in the country. Admittedly in a detached cottage of his own he could be as sober or as drunk as he pleased.

Hereward applied to an estate agent in Margate. One day he received particulars of a house in the street where Peggy lived. It seemed ideal, and to be going cheap, although Brownie was unselfishly opposed to the investment of such a large sum of money on his account.

Six months ago the price would have been unthinkable.

But in the meanwhile the Watkinses had sold 32 Trafalgar Terrace; and since they were already installed in Alice's flat in Suffolk Crescent, they did not need the cash for alternative accommodation. Thus Hereward had the chance at once to discharge his financial debt to Brownie, who had worked for him for a pittance through poorer years, and to shed the burden of those practical responsibilities which weighed on him more heavily than ever.

The little house in Margate, across the road from Peggy's, as it were sheltered by a family umbrella, would solve every problem – combined with some sort of pension.

Arguably, Brownie himself had supplied that solution by foiling Hereward's previous schemes for his welfare, just as he had created the problem in the first place. In his crafty fashion he had turned up his nose at a mansion in Hampstead and a high-class flatlet in South West One, and brought about the present concatenation of events from which he was likely to derive the maximum profit. From a cynical point of view he seemed to be on the verge of achieving his heart's desire by having behaved badly. His opposition to his boss's projected expenditure might have sprung from an ethical inkling that virtue, not vice, should be rewarded.

But Hereward was prepared to be pushed around as well as to push in the cause of a sort of emancipation. He had been constrained by his anxieties for too long. He had been punished enough for his happiness with Alice. He acknowledged that his marriage had wounded Brownie's competitive susceptibilities, perhaps chronically, whatever might be said to the contrary. He recalled that at the beginning of the last act of the drama he had pleaded for a postponement – a few weeks of peace in which to finish his current book. He now suspected that his pleading had been Brownie's chief incentive to wage total alcoholic war, even at the cost of his health and his job, in order to distract or attract his boss's attention.

They had traversed the charted areas of service, friendship, and assumptions of mastery on Brownie's side – and in a sense were locked in combat in a dark and barren no-man's-land. Hereward was willing to pay any ransom to get out of it.

Moreover he still wanted to keep his promise. In principle and on paper, each of his post-nuptial experiments had been better for Brownie than the one before. The little house would be the best. It could not be improved upon.

And after all the grudging part of Brownie's ambivalence was beneath the surface. It existed, it had expressed itself in action, and was perhaps not to be wondered at, and justifiable. But it was subterranean and possibly subconscious. He had scarcely uttered a single resentful word, and never scoffed or sneered at his boss's invidious marital state. And Hereward was aware that in an emergency, or if he were to suffer a setback, he – and his wife – could again count on Brownie's absolute and infinite devotion. He had enjoyed the unique privilege of being the object of that devotion for nearly a third of a century. He could not forget that Brownie had saved his bacon by painting the maisonette at Windle Road in a fortnight. He remembered how good Brownie had been to him when he was ill at Trafalgar Terrace, and the myriad jokes cracked by Brownie that had kept his melancholy at bay, and the mountains of Brownie's food he had eaten with relish, and the blessings Brownie had showered on his literary career, and the perennial fun they had had together.

The little house and the wherewithal to live in it was the very least he could do in return.

Brownie, informed of the decision of Hereward and Alice,

was overcome by gratitude, scolded them for their kindness, said goodbye and departed for Margate.

*

He was always a lucky devil.

But then his luck was merited by his moral qualities – setting aside his weakness for a bottle. In fact his courtship of fortune was usually successful more because he was careless of the outcome, was ready to do without fortune's favours, than because he was machiavellian. He got the things he wanted by not wanting them unduly – and never asking for them.

Thus it was with the little house, where the Watkinses hoped he would be happy, too.

He had to hang around for three months before he could obtain possession of it.

His first letters in his curlicued writing were extravagantly positive. 'Darling Madame and dearest Master – you are a pair of solid gold bricks . . .' He was staying with Peggy, feeding like a fighting cock, walking for miles along the sea-front in the early mornings, playing with his grandchildren whose sweets and treats were breaking the bank, and having the time of his life.

But soon he wrote from a different address. He was no longer staying with Peggy, who did not really have room for him. He was in temporary lodgings, not seeing much of his family, having difficulty in finding employment, and feeling the pinch : he was unaccustomed to having to pay his way, since his weekly wage for thirty years had been pocket money. The only job he had been offered was looking after the deck-chairs on the beach – he added exclamation marks to this sentence and underlined it ironically. Gentlemen's gentlemen of his age, and top chefs, were not required in Margate.

He was trying to draw the dole. In the past he had waxed violent on the subject of Social Security scroungers. Yet almost in the same breath he would say: 'When I'm on my uppers, I'll bleed that Social Security white! I'm entitled, Master – I fought and rotted in prison for my country – I'm not a lazy layabout . . .'

He had set about bleeding it. His references to what he was up to were contradictory. He had extracted a couple of pounds from the welfare people, he was getting a tenner a week, he had got fifteen pounds, he had been invited to dinner by the nice lady in charge of such handouts, who thought he was a most deserving case – and evidently had no idea that he was receiving an adequate pension from Hereward. Nevertheless he was not making ends meet, he wrote. He was having to economise all round – his weekly subsidy from the state was a mingy seven pounds and fifty pence. He was often hungry, and bored, and hated having nothing to do, and pined for his master and mistress.

He in his turn had not forgotten how to play upon his ex-boss's anxious affections. He had twisted his ankle on one of his walks – his leg had swollen to the size of a bolster. He was afraid he was growing old: he took to signing his letters, 'Your obedient old servant'. He rang Hereward constantly to enquire: 'Any worries or troubles, Master?' – a question designed to cause dismay, considering it meant that he was worried and troubled, and he only asked it when tipsy.

At last he was able to move into his house.

The proprietorship of property on a small scale is invariably good for the soul. The plaintive correspondence and nagging telephone calls ceased. After three or four weeks Brownie wrote: 'My dear Madame and Master – Sorry I haven't been in touch – I've been on the go from dawn until late at night – My new house is a miracle . . .'

At about the same time Hereward met a friend of his, Nancy Creston, who was eager for news of Brownie. Formerly Lady Creston had been a favoured client – Brownie used to say he could gobble her up – and she reciprocated his special feelings for her, if less carnivorously. Now, when she heard he was out of a job, she wanted to offer him one.

'Do you think he might come to my rescue, even for a day or two a week?'

She was a gentle sensitive person, abstemious yet tolerant, aware of his proclivities, under no illusions, convinced she could control him, or anyway that the effort of attempting to was worthwhile.

She contacted Brownie, whose response was eagerly affirmative.

Again that summer the Watkinses went abroad for three months.

'Dear Madame and Master,' ran the letter that awaited them on their return. 'Trusting you are both fit, as I am. I've settled into my house, which is the best in the street. I keep it regimental, not a spot of dust, wood floors polished so you can see your face in them – and I'm painting it bit by bit. Last week I bought a clock that charms for my lounge – half price – fell off the back of a lorry, I suppose. And I got my three-piece suite, settee and two comfy chairs – can't wait for you to try them. I've been travelling up to town to help Lady Creston Tuesdays and Thursdays. Her Ladyship takes a lot of beating – she is A1. My room there is gorgeous and I sleep between sheets with a coronet on them!! We have great jokes together, and she asks her family in for meals, and they all think I'm the pig's whiskers. The extra money is handy. And I still touch my other lady from the Social Security – not what you're thinking, sir!! So I'm quite flush for the present. At weekends I blitz my house, do the shopping, see my grand-children, and lean on the garden gate, smoking my pipe and chewing the cud with neighbours. Dear Madame and Master, you have done me proud. I know I was wicked and should have been shot. Instead you've given me everything I ever dreamt of. I don't know how to say thank you ...'

Hereward spoke to Brownie on the telephone.

'You seem to be well?'

'I was never better, sir.'

'And the house is a success?'

'It's a smash-hit – and keeps me out of mischief.'

'And your arrangements with Lady Creston suit you?'

'Down to the ground.'

'I'm so glad.'

'Any chance of seeing you, sir?'

'Come round when you're next in London.'

'What about Tuesday? I could cook lunch for yourself and Madame. Her Ladyship isn't expecting me till the afternoon.'

'That'd be a pleasure for us.'

'No, no, sir – my pleasure. I'll look forward to it.'

'Same here, Brownie.'

On Tuesday he did not arrive at the appointed hour. The engagement could have slipped his mind, or maybe there had been a muddle about which week he was coming round. Hereward clung to such sanguine explanations until the evening, when Nancy Creston rang to tell him Brownie was missing. They drew the disappointing conclusion that he had relapsed alcoholically: they could not communicate with anyone and make sure, since neither he nor Peggy had tele-phones in their respective homes.

The next day they sent him a telegram, to which they received no reply. They had been reluctant to sneak on him to his daughter; but now they disregarded their scruples to the extent of sending a telegram to Peggy, who reported back that her father's house seemed empty. Four days passed. They were unwilling to inform the police for fear of the scandal that would finish Brownie if he was found to be merely drunk in some ditch or gutter. No doubt the members of his family were restrained for similar reasons – and because they believed he must be misbehaving in London. Then Hereward sent a third telegram to Peggy. Brownie was discovered dead on the floor of his kitchen.

He had died of a heart attack, instantaneously, and probably on the preceding Tuesday morning, for he was clasping his railway return ticket to London in his hand.

Innumerable doctors had fussed over his tumours and his liver. Not one had noticed that his heart was in a perilous condition.

He had fooled the medical profession for the last time – and Hereward for that matter. To put it another way, Hereward had failed to see through his final deception. But who was to say whether Brownie marched through the pearly gates drunk or sober, or as a direct consequence of his having had his last one too many? His death was as ambiguous and secretive as his life.

It was all very sudden and sad. He was too young to die at sixty-three or sixty-four or however old he was – mentally youthful and vital at any rate.

The compensating factor was that his luck had held good.

When he died he was not a boozy casualty of the class struggle, used and discarded, sacked and in disgrace, with nothing to show for his fifty years of kind service except Carpet Feet and the shakes, unable to adapt to retirement and the ageing processes, a burden to his friends and relations, a victim of his own stupidity – but a householder, a man of means and substance, still on the best of terms with his boss who had cared for him enough to make his dreams come true, forgiven as he forgave, perhaps enjoying himself more than ever before, looking forward to his future, and at work, in harness, just as he had wished.

So in a sense the comedy had its happy ending.